Promise Me
You Will
Find them

Nedra enjoy

Anna

Anna L. Kearns

NEWMAN SPRINGS PUBLISHING
320 Broad Street
Red Bank, NJ 07701

First originally published by Newman Springs Publishing 2020

ISBN 978-1-64801-872-5 (Paperback)
ISBN 978-1-64801-873-2 (Digital)

Printed in the United States of America

I dedicate this book to my wonderful
family who put up with the many
hours I spent at the computer.

CONTENTS

....

CHAPTER ONE

....

Murder and Frostbite

MY NAME IS AMELIA Wright, but I prefer to go by my nickname Amy. I work for the Seattle Homicide Department as a detective. A few months ago, I was promoted, and it was my dream come true. To tell you the truth, I can't remember a time I wasn't playing the role of a police officer. My brother, sister, and I played cops and robbers with all the neighborhood kids. I loved reading mysteries when I was young. I was always trying to solve the them before I got to the end of the book. I'll tell you a secret: I still love reading good mysteries, but now I get to solve real crimes.

Early this morning, I got a call from our lieutenant telling me I would be the lead detective on a new case. He told me to get to the crime scene fast. This is my first lead case. I'm assuming the lieutenant wants to see if I can handle the stress, long hours, and huge amount of work involved in solving a case. I pray I'm up to the task.

We are experiencing horrible snow and extreme cold weather right now. Knowing this will help you understand what the homicide officers are up against.

Seattle is known throughout the country for being extremely rainy but not for subzero temperatures. Everyone, even the cops who have walked their beats for years, won't stay out very long. Officers driving patrol cars won't venture far from them. The cars are left running while the officers run carefully to check out stores. And that is only if something looks suspicious. Getting frostbite isn't high on anyone's priority list!

The lieutenant told me the body of a woman was spotted in a parking lot downtown on Fifth Avenue near Stewart Street. On my way to the crime scene, I was thinking this horrible weather might have factored into her going unnoticed until this morning as I was told she had been there a while. Because of the weather, I was driving about twenty miles an hour. That was the top speed I felt safe doing. Normally, I would be going a lot faster.

The lieutenant told me Mike Bowers, another detective, would be assisting me. He was at the crime scene when I arrived. Mike is a veteran, and I'm so glad he is helping. He saw me and said, "Hi, Amy, what took you so long?" I just glared at him then smiled and said, "Wiseass." He just snickered.

We walked over to one of the officer who arrived at the crime scene before us. He told us her body was found next to a car in the lot. "She is at the back in this dark, dinky parking lot," he said with disgust. Probably this was the biggest reason she wasn't noticed earlier. Looking at the lot, it is narrow with only enough room for cars to park on one side. It literally runs from the front of the building to the alley behind. It is visible from the street, but if you are doing the speed limit or not familiar with the area, you will miss it.

"We've already searched the area around the body, but there wasn't a purse or any other form of identification. On top of that, the car next to her was locked," the officer said. "If it were unlocked, we could have checked the registration to find out who she was. We need to know who she is or, at this point, was. Now the legwork begins."

Let me back up a little as it will help you to get a clear picture of the crime scene I came to. When I saw Victoria's body, I lost what little breakfast I had managed to eat before I left my apartment. I tried to hide it, but I knew I wasn't successful. There were, however, quite a few gag reflexes on the faces of other officers after they viewed her body. It took a moment to calm my rolling stomach and start doing my job. I didn't want to let anyone down who was involve in solving this horrendous crime.

We headed into the business adjacent to the cars. The crime scene guys took a picture of the side of her face that was visible for us to use. We took it with us in hopes we could find out who she is. The picture didn't turn out very good. We would have liked it to be better, but because of the poor lighting and glare from the snow, it wasn't perfect. Using a flash doesn't always work when it is dark, and there is bright white snow around. We had to use it anyway. Something is better than nothing. Right?

We entered the building and approached the receptionist. I handed her the photo and asked her if she knew the victim. After looking at the picture, she said it might be Victoria Clump. Although she wasn't sure, she added. We asked her to please take another look. We knew the picture wasn't good, but we had to try. She looked at it again and thought for another minute. Then said for the second time it might be her. She added Victoria had worked late the night before. Her last statement led us to believe she was only guessing. We need to have a better than a guess ID. I asked if she knew what kind of car Victoria drove. She answered yes. I gave her the description of the car next to the body. She emphatically said that is Victoria's car.

Hallelujah! We have an ID, I thought. Although a poor one.

Mike asked the receptionist why the parking lot didn't have better lighting. She said Mr. Wilde, the owner of the Wilde Company, didn't replace the lights until they were all burned out. Or almost all of them. He was known around the company as Mr. Tightwad.

That is a good moniker, I thought.

Since the lot was very poorly lit, I surmised that Ms. Clump might have hurried to her car, not seeing someone lurking in the shadows. The dark and cold certainly let someone get close enough to attack her.

Going back to the lot, a crime scene tech met us and told us that Mr. Wilde found her early that morning. He pointed him out. Victoria, if that was actually who she was, wasn't a pretty sight, and we noticed Mr. Wilde was still a little green from finding her. I hope being cheap will haunt him for a very long time. We headed over to him and began asking questions.

I asked him to describe what happened when he arrived. He told us he parked in his usual spot and was surprised to see Victoria's car still there and the snow on it wasn't disturbed. So he walked back to have a look around and found her lying there. He said he got very queasy but managed to shakily dial 911, reported her body, and gave the address. He told us he didn't have time to tell the 911 operator her name because he was gagging too much. He hung up and hurried into the building to throw up. He then waited for the police to arrive. He didn't go back outside as it was too cold. We left him for a minute to talk with another officer. Mike told him, as we were walking away, "We will be back to get more information." He just glared and shivered.

We went over to talk with Officer Jeff Davis. He said when he and the others arrived, Mr. Wilde was in bad shape. They called Medic One for they feared "Mr. Tightwad" was having a mild heart attack. Everyone was calling him that because of the near nonexistent lights in the lot. I didn't feel sorry for him. Again, my spidey senses were screaming at me if the lights had been replaced she would have seen someone lurking. She could have run out to the street and yelled for help. As it was, she didn't have a fighting chance back there.

We headed back to talk with Mr. Wilde before he was taken to the hospital. The first thing he said, "Do I need my attorney?" We told him this was just a preliminary talk. He then said okay. We asked where he was the night Victoria was killed. He begrudgingly told us he left his business at 7:15 p.m. to go home. It was like pulling teeth to get that out of him. He continued to be reluctant to give us anything. We then asked for Victoria's address and next of kin. He told us to meet with Ms. Hastings in Human Resources. She would have Victoria's info on file. We asked what his company did. He explained that the Wilde Company is a shoe design and manufacturing company. We asked why Victoria had what looked like a new boot on, notice boot. He said he wanted to promote his new line of winter dress boots, so he gave a pair to all the female salesladies. Victoria was wearing the newly designed boots all day yesterday. That was the same day she was murdered. He told us she was working when he left, and she still had the boots on. She was probably wearing them when she was killed. I was wondering where the other boot was because it wasn't in the lot.

He was able to identify Victoria by the high-top boot and by her red hair. This was the positive ID we needed. He added that was all he was going to say he needed to go to the hospital. Before the Medics took Mr. Wilde to Harborview Hospital, a highly rated trauma center, we wanted to ask more questions; but he gave us a lot of attitude and didn't want to answer any more questions. His last statement was, "I need to be checked out, I feel awful." I was sure he didn't feel as awful as Victoria had felt. I wanted to slap him up alongside of his head, but that would have been considered police brutality. I had to walk away quickly before I actually did it.

Back to Victoria, my guess was she had probably been attractive. Half of her face had been bashed in, so I really couldn't say for sure. She was about 5'8" tall and weighed around 120 pounds. Her hair was red by nature. She was dressed haphazardly, which didn't fit as her clothes looked expensive. She had frostbite on the extremities that were visible. I thought the assailant or assailants were either very strong or strung out on drugs. We were all sure of the cause of death. It was blunt force trauma, but an autopsy would be performed anyway to confirm how she was murdered.

The crime scene unit finished taking pictures. We were hoping these were better than the first one. They gathered what little evidence there was and left. Right after they pulled out, the coroner's van arrived. We weren't surprised it took them a while to get here. Even with numerous sanding trucks working as hard as they could, nothing was moving very fast in the city.

To understand why it took so long for the coroner to get to us, you have to know about driving here in winter. Seattle is pretty treacherous to navigate because of the many steep hills especially when they are covered with ice and snow. Several years ago, a visiting Midwest basketball team found out the hard way. They wanted to go into the center of the city before they left for home. They were warned not to use the hilly course they chose as it was too dangerous. They decided since they drove in snow all winter long, it wouldn't be a problem. They went down a steep hill from the Capitol Hill area.

They ended up sliding down and teetering on a retaining wall above Interstate 5, commonly called I-5. People assume driving in snow here is the same as it is in the Midwest. No, it isn't. If they are ever here again in winter, I'm sure they will listen when told their route isn't safe. Even when it rains hard, your tires spin on the steep hills.

Ugh, I hate snow and cold weather! It isn't like this very often, but when it is, I wonder why I am still here. Then I think to myself you know why, because you really love it here. I wouldn't live anywhere else. This state is so beautiful and has so much to offer. There is skiing, tubing, and snowboarding in the mountains in winter. You can go swimming or sailing on Puget Sound or on the many lakes in the summer. You can camp at different parks or on the beaches. There are hiking and biking trails all over the state. If you don't like those activities there are theaters, museums, parks, golf courses, horse racing, sporting events, and other amusements. I can't leave out the numerous great restaurants. If you don't like the evergreen side of the state, you can drive across the mountains to the hot dry part of the state. You can go camping or wind surfing on the Columbia river and lakes. You can also do a lot of the activities mentioned above. I can't forget to mention the great fishing on both sides of the state. I tell myself get back to the crime scene.

Coroner Ben Saunders had been working the graveyard shift at Harborview and hadn't been relieved yet. He was tired and in no mood to stand out in the freezing weather. He didn't talk much and worked as quickly as possible to get what he needed. The body was lifted onto the gurney and into the van for transport to the morgue. Even though it was freezing, Ben was still being through. He took one last look around to make sure he didn't miss anything or leave something behind. With this accomplished, they took off.

I considered going into forensic medicine but changed my mind. I decided I would do better with a criminology degree. After seeing Victoria and losing my stomach contents, I'm positive I wouldn't have been any good in a morgue. At this moment, I know it was the best decision I ever made.

We had wrapped everything up and headed to the station. After freezing, I was ready to get warm. I also wanted to get something in my empty stomach. We all drove as fast as we could back to the station. I couldn't help it, I stopped to get a scone and a cup of coffee at the corner Starbucks. I parked in the garage and headed up to the squad room. When I entered, I was immediately met with the strains to "There She Is Miss America" only the words were changed to here she comes Ms. Throw-up Queen. The song didn't bother me, as it let me know I was accepted as part of the team.

I was really thankful for the warmth in the squad room. I sat down at my desk and looked at Mike with a sheepish smiled. He knew how horrible it was, so he didn't say a word. Every officer there had to squelch their nausea. I told him I was grateful to have him help me solve this case. He just smiled.

Let me explain why I was so grateful for his help. Mike has been in the department five years and has an excellent apprehension record. I really, really want to solve this one. So, I want and need all the help the lieutenant can give me.

I was finally thawing out. Although it seemed like as soon as I sat down we were summoned to the lieutenant's office. I grabbed my scone and coffee and headed in there. Jim Nickels is our lieutenant, and there isn't a better one in the entire force. He wanted to go over what we learned from the crime scene. There wasn't much to give him except the knowledge that Mr. Wilde was the last person to see Victoria alive, and he was a douche. I didn't say that out loud, but I'm sure after we continued working on this case everyone would have the same opinion of Mr. Tightwad.

Luckily Ben, the coroner, called right then. Jim put him on speaker, and he told us he that Victoria had been raped and brutally beaten to death. She was alive when the rape occurred as there were signs she had put up a struggle. She managed to scratch her assailant and skin was under some of her nails. While struggling, she also broke off a couple of nails. He was sure they weren't at the crime scene. Ben couldn't say for sure where the assailant was scratched, but the skin didn't have any hair follicles. This indicated the perpetrator wouldn't have scratches on his face. He said they were running the skin fragments through the DNA database to see if there was a match.

The time of death couldn't be pinpointed because of the extreme cold, but he thought it had happened sometime between 8:30 to 10:30 p.m.

Whoever committed this crime had to be desperate to perform a rape in subzero weather. I hoped he had some frostbite on his derriere not to mention the frontal portion of his anatomy. Ben said Rhonda, his replacement, was finally there. He was going home to get some much needed sleep, but before he hung up, he added, "I'll get back with you when I return. I don't want anyone else touching this case. You know my boundaries." We said okay, what else were we supposed to do. We trusted him. He was one of the best coroners, and he was headed home for some well-deserved time off.

We resumed our discussion with the lieutenant. I told him my suspicion that it was a drug-related act. Drug addicts don't have the brains God gave a flea. Jim and Mike nodded in agreement. Mike and Jim started talking again. My mind started going on to other things. I wondered if Victoria was abducted, driven somewhere else, then dumped back in the lot? That would account for the amount of blood, or lack of. Also, where were the missing fingernails and boot? Or maybe someone she knew picked her up. I let these scenarios simmer in my mind and decided to share them when there was a lull in their conversation.

I told them what I had been mulling over. The lieutenant and Mike agreed these were possibilities. We shared more ideas and agreed there were several possibilities, but right now, all we had were just that, possibilities.

Jim said to find out as much as we could about Victoria. We didn't need to be told to do this; we already knew it. We told him we planned on going over to meet with workers at the Wilde Company. I added I want to see if anything out of the ordinary is going on. I really have a gut instinct about that place. Mike said, "What gut? I don't see any gut." I glared and poked him in the arm. Jim just laughed and said, "Go with that instinct. Sometimes they are the best."

We were getting ready to leave when I remembered we hadn't shared our brief but useless interview with Mr. Wilde. I said, "We didn't tell you all about our interview with Mr. Wilde." I said, "He didn't give us much information and was very uncooperative. He even asked if he should have his attorney present. We had to assured him we only needed basic information. Then he reluctantly agreed to talk to us. He definitely didn't want to say something that might incriminate him. It made me wonder what was really going on. Jim thought it very strange he didn't want to help find his employee's killer. I have my suspicions about Mr. Wilde, and I guess that is why my gut is telling me something stinks." Mike said he agreed with my assessment.

"Jim told us to notify Victoria's next of kin before we went back to the Wilde Company. It helps them if they get the news from us. In a way, they have a shoulder to cry on, so to speak. He especially didn't want them to hear about it on the evening news. You can go to the Wild Company after that," he added. We agreed.

Notifying the family is the most unpleasant job we have. You don't want see the pain and suffering it causes them. But it is a necessary duty. In fact, it is the hardest part of this job. I was given this task on one occasion, and it was extremely hard for me to do it.

Again, we were in the process of leaving the office when Jim told us to meet with Mrs. Wilde too. He said to make sure she can verify Mr. Wilde's story. Especially since he was so unwilling to be interviewed.

"That is an understatement," I said. With that, Mike and I left.

Coming out of the office, we were met by Jeff and some of the crime scene boys. They told us they were able to get some good tire impressions from the parking lot. They indicated there were three different sets of impressions around Victoria's car. Jeff said it looks like one came from a pretty expensive foreign car. Possibly a Jaguar or a Ferrari. We thanked them for this info. It gave us something to be on the lookout for.

Luckily, it hadn't snowed after 7:00 p.m. "We need to find out what car Mr. Wilde drove yesterday as he left work after the last snowfall. We also need to know if he has more than one car just in case he came back," I said. "We knew Victoria's car hadn't moved as the snow around it was not disturbed. The expensive sports car could be our biggest lead. Or I should say, the only one we had so far."

We followed Mr. Wilde's curt instructions to get Victoria's information from Ms. Hastings. We called the company and was connected with her. We asked her for Victoria's next of kin information and her home address. She able to give us her next of kin's address along with their telephone number. She also gave us the address where Victoria lived. She added if you need anything else, I will be available to help.

We now knew where Victoria's parents lived. "I'm not looking forward to this," I said as we got in Mike's car.

He said, "You need to get used to doing this, Amy."

"I know," I said. "But that doesn't make it any easier. Or make me want to do it."

CHAPTER TWO

....

The Bad News and More Questions

MIKE AND I DROVE to Mercer Island where the Clumps lived. We wanted to get the hardest part over with and not run the risk of them hearing of Victoria's death on the news or some other way. We arrived at about 2:30 p.m. Mr. and Mrs. Clump were home as they didn't want to venture out in the crappy weather. I wish more Seattleites and other affected community residents would adopt this attitude. It would certainly eliminate a lot of traffic accidents, not to mention numerous insurance claims.

We introduced ourselves. I said, "We have some very bad news to tell you." They looked at each other and got teary-eyed. We found out later they had only one child, and they were sure it had something to do with Victoria. We told them their daughter had been murdered. Of course they broke down. After a short while, they composed themselves.

We asked a couple of basic questions to break some of the tension. We learned that Victoria worked at company and going to college in the evenings to get her nursing degree. She had an associate degree in business, but after volunteering at a Hospice Center, she decided to change her curriculum over to nursing.

Mrs. Clump added that Victoria was engaged to Andy Matthews. They planned to announce their engagement on Valentine's Day.

That was just a couple of weeks away. They were planning their wedding for next year. Victoria wanted to graduate before they married. Then she would only have to concentrate on one event at a time.

We asked them about Victoria's acquaintances. Mrs. Clump said she knew of several and left to make us a list of her friends. When she returned, she said her daughter didn't talk about the people she worked with much so they weren't on the list. She asked if that was a problem. We assured her it wasn't.

Then Mr. Clump started to talk about Andy. He said Andy was attending college to get his law degree at the University of Washington. He was happy Victoria had found him. Andy was really in love with her and always treated her with respect and affection. I asked the Clumps if they would rather have us tell Andy the bad news, but they insisted they should. They reasoned, "Andy had no relatives close by, and we were almost family so we would let him know."

We wanted a chance to chat with Andy too. So I asked if we could be there when they told him. Right away, they agreed to call us when they knew what time he was coming to their house. I know their wanting us there was based on having support. Dealing with death is never an easy task. Dealing with murder is almost impossible. I asked if there was anything else we could do before we left. They asked to see their daughter. Mike looked away grimacing. Knowing my reaction to seeing Victoria, I strongly suggested they wait.

Mike told them an autopsy was required when it was a murder investigation, and one was being done now. We knew it was already done, but this was the easiest way to save them extra pain right now. I couldn't bring myself to explain to them how she looked when we arrived at the crime scene. I didn't want to upset them further.

To change the subject, I said, "Please don't go over to Victoria's apartment yet. We need to see if there is anything out of the ordinary there." They said they would wait as it would be too hard to go there now anyway. Mike and I said, "Good. We will call you when it is okay for you to go to Victoria's."

When we were leaving, Mrs. Clump took a hold of my arm and said, "Find the person responsible for killing our little girl. Promise me you will find them!" I said we would do our utmost to find her killer. We added our condolences, gave them our business cards, and left.

Since we were not far from Bellevue, we headed to the Wildes' residence instead of heading back to the station. The Somerset district of Bellevue is not that far from Mercer Island. The Wildes' residence was near the top of Somerset, and it was beautiful. The homes at the top are really expensive. As a matter of fact, most homes in Bellevue are very expensive. There are areas where homes are normal, but everyone thinks people living in Bellevue have a lot of money.

We took a chance Mrs. Wilde would be there. She was home and agreed to meet with us but only for a little bit. She explained she had an appointment that couldn't be put off even with the horrible weather. A cab was on its way to pick her up as Mr. Wilde had the four-wheel drive Escalade. She didn't want to drive the other vehicles in this weather. We asked her what other cars they owned. She replied they have an older Jaguar sedan and a Lincoln Town Car.

We asked her what time Mr. Wilde arrived home last night. She told us he got home right around 8:20 p.m. or maybe a little later, but her favorite program was on and it was more than halfway over. It usually takes thirty to forty minutes to drive to Somerset from Seattle in normal rush hour traffic, so the time was about right considering the weather conditions. We asked if she had heard anything that might have led to Victoria being murdered. She didn't know why someone would want to harm her. Her exact words were, "She was such a nice girl. Why would anyone want to hurt her?" We thanked Mrs. Wilde for her time, left her our business cards, and headed out.

Hearing what time Mr. Wilde arrive home, we knew there wasn't time for him to commit the murder. Darn, I was secretly hoping it was him. He was such a big weasel. Plus, he gave me the willies.

On our way back to the station, I thought, what a huge waste. Why kill someone who had so much going for them? She seemed to be a nice young woman. What a horrible way for your life to end. Mrs. Clump's request kept running through my mind. I made a mental promise that I would do everything I could to find the psycho or psychos and make them pay dearly for this crime.

When we got in the car, I checked my cell. I left as I didn't want it ringing when we were talking with Mrs. Wilde. There was one message from the station. Luckily, I wasn't driving, so I put it on speaker so Mike could hear it too. The message was from Dale. He said he answered my phone and it was Mrs. Clump. Her message was, she was successful in leaving Andy a message with his room-mate. Andy wasn't home. She asked Mr. Olson to tell Andy they wanted him to come over for an early dinner. Here is the short ver-sion: the roommate gave Andy the message when he got home. Andy called them and said he would be on his way as soon as he changed.

Hope the message was helpful. I looked at Mike and he said, "Since we are headed toward Mercer Island, we'll go there."

I dialed their number. Mr. Clump answered. I said, "This is detective Amy Wright. We got Mrs. Clump's message and are on our way to your home."

He said, "Good. We will be looking for you."

With the trips between Seattle to Mercer Island, to Bellevue and then back to Mercer Island, we had no problem getting there fairly fast. We definitely wanted get there before Andy showed up.

When we arrived, the Clumps were looking out the window. They opened the door as we were walking up the sidewalk. They said they were glad we made such good time. We told them, "We were in Somerset and on our way back to the station when we got your message." They said Andy asked why Victoria hadn't called after getting home from her night class; she usually called so he wouldn't worry. The Clumps told him they would find out and let him know what happened. They also said he had been cramming for an exam last night. When he quit studying, he saw how late it was, so he didn't want to disturb her. He just went to bed. I think the Clumps are the nicest people to worry about his feelings when they were so distraught.

Andy arrived soon after us. He looks like I had pictured him in my mind; average height, maybe 5'10" tall, with dark hair and he was nice-looking. Not my type, but I could see how he would appeal to another woman. I like men who are tall and well-built. I guessed he was about three years older than Victoria. He didn't react to our news like the Clumps did. No tears, no anger, no emotion whatsoever. I thought how strange to act as nothing had happened.

On top of that, his answers to our questions were delivered as if they had been rehearsed. Then I thought maybe it was because he was going to be an attorney. Yah, that could be the reason for his reaction. Darn, my mind was in going in all directions again. Why do I do this? I made a mental note to ask Mike about his behavior when we got back to the car.

Back on track, I asked him what type of law he was leaning toward. He said he had a year and a half left and hadn't quite decided yet. He was considering corporate law or being a prosecuting attorney. Hmm, two different sides of the law. I thought, with so little time left before you graduate wouldn't you have chosen what type of the law you want to practice? Aren't there courses geared to those sides of the law? I asked myself.

While I was mulling over his remarks, Mike asked if his roommate would be up to answering some questions. Andy got real hostile and demanded to know what we wanted to talk with him for. Mike calmly told him that people who weren't close to the victim could possibly remember some odd coincidence that might lead to something. The explanation seemed to appease him, and he gave us Duncan Olson's phone number. I guess they didn't share expenses. We asked some more questions. We had as much as we were going to get, so we gave our condolences again and left.

On the way to the car, I remembered Officer Jeff's comment that one of the tire prints belonged to an expensive foreign car. I made sure to see what kind of car he was driving. Wouldn't you know it, it was an older Ford Explorer. Somehow this vehicle wasn't exactly what I expected to see him driving. His persona didn't match the SUV type. He was too uptight and uppity.

I guess I don't like the attorney type. Some I've dealt with were such dirtbags. Some others thought they were above me. That doesn't sit well with me either. So, either way, I don't have much use for them. Maybe one day I'll meet an attorney I like and that is a big maybe.

When we were in the car, I commented on Andy's lack of emotion when learning about his fiancée's murder. Mike said people reacted in different ways to information like this. He had seen this behavior before. He said Andy might breakdown when he gets to his apartment, or it could possibly take longer. He suggested we mention this to his roommate when we interviewed him. It would give him a heads-up of what might be coming down the pike for Andy. I called from the car and Mr. Olson was home. I told him we needed to speak with him regarding his roommate. He said to come on over and gave us his address.

There were ten apartments listed on the registry for the entire building. I was thinking this building is quite large for just ten apartments. Mike interrupted my thoughts by saying Duncan's name is on the registry but not Andy's. That's strange, maybe it was because he moved in later. Mike pushed the intercom to let him know we had arrived. Duncan answered and told us to come on up. His apartment was indeed very large with open living areas. Nice but not extravagant. Knowing the area the building was located in and the size of the apartment, it was pricey just the same.

Duncan was older than Andy by a couple of years and more my type. He had sandy-blond hair and blue eyes. He stood about 6'2" with broad shoulders and outstanding looks. I warned myself to get my mind back on the case. I asked if he was going to college and he laughed. It was very pleasant. Something I would like to hear more often and could get used to. Darn, get back to why we are here, I told myself.

When we told Duncan the reason we were there, he said what a bummer she was killed. It is sad for young people to lose their lives. I'm really sorry it happened to her. He added, "Andy…He really loved her." He said Andy told him they were engaged, but they hadn't officially announced it. He was told not to say anything yet, which was okay with him.

I asked Duncan what he did for a living just out of curiosity. He told us he was a freelance photographer. I asked if some of the pictures hanging around the apartment were his. He nodded yes. To get back on the subject, Mike asked if Andy was paying for half the rent.

Duncan laughed and said he is just renting a bed and bath while he goes to college. I asked if he knew Andy before he rented him the rooms. "No," he replied. A friend told him Andy was looking for a quiet room where he could study and sleep. He also wanted a private bathroom. "He was a nice kid, so I offered him one of the spare bedrooms and a bathroom I didn't use." Duncan added, "I charge him a nominal rental fee as I was just being nice." He added, "I don't need the income." I wonder what he meant by not needing the income. Hmm?

We asked how Duncan met Victoria. He said he was doing a photo shoot at the Wilde Company and met her there. I asked how he got that job. He said one of his clients recommended him to Mr. Wilde. The Wilde Company did a lot of advertising, and he was glad to be part of their new campaign. Duncan said Andy asked if he could go with him to earn some extra money. He agreed as extra help was always welcome.

Duncan said when he first met Victoria, he wasn't impressed with her at all. He followed that up with she tried to get him to go out with her, and she implied she would go all the way if he were willing to pay. His description wasn't flattering at all.

After he told her he wasn't looking for a connection, to put it nicely, she became interested in Andy. She wasn't keen on him when they first arrived. On the other hand, at first sight of Victoria, Andy was smitten with her.

We asked Duncan if Andy knew about her coming on to him. He said he wasn't sure. He thought Andy was nearby when Victoria said what she wanted him to do, but he couldn't swear to it. There was a lot going on and the noise level was pretty high. Displays were being set up and some of the models were selecting what shoes they were going to wear in the shoot. That was causing a lot of arguing since the models wanted to wear the same shoes.

I wasn't concentrating on the last part of the conversation. I was still caught up in the sexual favor scenario. Wow, this information painted a complete opposite view of Victoria.

Maybe that was why Mr. Wilde wasn't too willing to talk about her. Not everyone wants to speak poorly of the dead. It didn't bother

Duncan to talk freely about her. We asked if he had other occasions to socialize with Andy and Victoria. He answered several times, but Victoria had left him alone. He gave us a list of people and employees who were at parties they all attended. He also gave us a list of employees who were at each shoot, and of course, Mr. Wilde was at the top of each list.

Before we left, Mike informed Duncan that Andy might have a rough time when he gets back to his room. If not, then it might be at a later time. Duncan said he would keep an eye on him. We informed Duncan we might need to come by again for further information if necessary. We handed him our cards. He looked straight at me and said it wouldn't be a problem for us to come by at any time. We didn't even need to call first. I couldn't let Mike or Duncan for that matter see me blush. It just wasn't professional. I needed to get out in the freezing air before my face caught on fire. Oh my, I haven't blushed like this since I was a preteen.

I didn't realize until I was in the cold air that I was already looking forward to seeing Duncan Olson again. I wasn't able to figure out what was going on with this case or for that matter with me. I didn't think it would be a good idea to see Duncan anytime soon. Deep down, I really wanted to. He did suggest there was no problem with us coming by again, but there was too much smiling with maybe a little bit of a leer included. I know the leer was directed at me. Oh, brother, not again. I need to get things straightened out and get my head back on straight.

I finally got myself under control when we were in the car. Mike made a comment about our need to interview the people at the Wilde Company but added it is after 7:00 p.m. He didn't think anyone would or should be there. Neither one of us spoke after that. There was complete silence. I think we had talked ourselves into oblivion. I know I was done in. Mike drove directly to the station so I could get my car. I was totally in the mood to go home and climb into a hot, hot bath. I also needed to grab a bite to eat before my backbone was permanently part of my stomach. My second breakfast had been a long time ago.

When I had my car door open, I looked back at Mike and said this has certainly been a most unusual day. He agreed. I said, "Good night. I'll see you in the morning." Mike just nodded and drove out of the garage. He did a lot of that. A man of few words, kind of like Gary Cooper. In case you don't know him, he was an actor in old films. I really like him in the old Westerns.

I drove home and drug myself into my apartment. I headed directly to the bathroom and drew my bath. I really needed to get thawed out. The weather hadn't gotten any better. It was even colder tonight. Finally, my clothes were in a pile by the tub, and I was blissfully laying in hot water. While I was basking in the tub, I thought about the information we had learned today. I started to sort it out in my mind. The most perplexing thing is, who was Victoria? Was she the nice girl who was going to help cancer patients, or was she a professional call girl? If she was doing "extracurricular work" on the side, was it to pay for her college? I couldn't ask the Clumps these questions. They already lost their child. They didn't need to lose their good image of her. I would try my best to keep this information from them. I was thinking this was going to be a tall order.

If this side of Victoria was true, it would be difficult to hide. When this case goes to trial, that information would undoubtedly come out. Defense attorneys love to dig up as much dirt against the victim as they can. They believe it gives their client a reason for doing what they did. They don't care about the victim. All they want is keeping their client from getting convicted. It doesn't matter to them if it hurt the loved ones of the victim.

I tell myself enough of that. Right now, I need to get out of my bath, get some food in me, and then a good night's sleep. Since my bathwater was getting cold, it was easy to get out. I wrapped a warm robe around me and headed for the kitchen.

I had planned to go grocery shopping this morning. Because of the murder investigation, I didn't have time to make a grocery list or shop for that matter. I didn't expect to find much. Just as I thought there was little food in the refrigerator or in the cabinets. I found a few eggs and milk in the refrigerator and a loaf of whole wheat bread in the bread box. I made a fried egg sandwich and drank a tall glass of milk. That was good enough for now as my stomach was almost full. I promised myself I would make a grocery list in the morning. I stumbled into the bedroom, snuggled into my bed, and collapsed into a deep, deep sleep.

Mike called me at 7:30 in the morning. He fortunately caught me before I walk out the door. He told me he had to make a quick stop, and he would meet me at TWC (The Wilde Company). We decided to shorten it. Saying the full name of the company was so tiring and time-consuming. I asked what his arrival time might be. He thought around 8:30 a.m. I was a little curious about his quick stop, but I didn't ask what it was about. I headed out the door. Oh, darn, I forgot the grocery list again. No time for that now!

I arrived at TWC at 8:15 a.m. and looked around the parking lot. There weren't many cars. Hopefully, there will be someone in so I can start to interview.

When I entered the building, there was only the receptionist in the foyer. I asked if she had a few minutes to talk. She said it wasn't busy, so she could answer a few questions.

I asked if she ever heard any gossip going on around the office. She was very willing to fill me in on the company gossip. She informed me she had a little dirt on everyone. You can never hide something from a lonely person.

They love to live vicariously through other people's experiences.

I asked her about Mr. Wilde. She said he was a womanizer, and he put the make on almost every woman in the company. I asked her to give me their names. They were all the salesladies, including Victoria and some others.

To be nice, I asked if she had been approached and she quickly said, "Heavens no." She didn't give out that sort of vibe. I asked her what kind of vibe she was talking about. Her response was, "You know, when a woman dresses a certain way, casts those glances, and basically rubs up against the man she wants to get to know better." It was hard to keep a straight face. She was so demonstrative while explaining what she meant. I asked her if all the women on her list fit this description. She answered with a quick yes! I was curious about her response as I didn't find Mr. Wilde appealing at all. I didn't buy into this.

If it were true, then there were certainly a lot of loose women at TWC. I wondered if it was a prerequisite for being hired. Some of the names on the list she gave me I hadn't heard before. Maybe they no longer worked here. I didn't get to question her further as Mr. Wilde arrived and roughly grabbed my arm while angrily asking why I was bothering his help. I was lucky as Mike entered the building at almost the same time. He said in an very authoritative voice to let go of her before he was arrested for harming an officer of the law.

Mr. Wilde let me go just as quickly as he had grabbed my arm. Let me describe Mike so you know why Mr. Wilde did so. Mike is an extremely good-looking reincarnation of the Hulk, without being a green monster of course. He is 6'4" inches tall and weighs around 230 pounds, which is all hard muscle. He is part Hawaiian and part Caucasian with light brown hair and brown eyes. Really not hard to look at either if you know what I mean.

Mike escorted Mr. Wilde to a corner of the reception area away from the front desk. He told him to take us to his office or a conference room so we could talk in private. I guess his wife told him we talked, and she confirmed his alibi as he didn't protest about being interrogated this time. He quickly walked off down the hallway with us scurrying behind. I should say I was scurrying. We passed by the conference room and went straight to his office. I love seeing Mike intimidate people without raising a finger. I need to work on my technique. I'm only 5'5" inches tall in my bare feet and weigh 110 pounds on a good day, so I don't see me intimidating anyone soon. Oh well, I can dream, can't I?

When we were seated in his office, we started on our list of questions. Mike started with a few basic ones. When it was my turn, I asked him what cars he owned. Was he faithfully married, or did he have extramarital affairs with his female employees. He jumped up and exploded. He yelled that was none of my business. Especially the last question. He was red in the face and angry as a bull who just had a red cape swirled in its face.

Mike very slowly stood up and said, "Sit down. Calm down and answer Detective Wright's questions." I guess he was only able to bully women as he sat down and started to talk. He answered the question about his cars. He said he had a Lincoln Town Car, an older Jaguar sedan, and an Escalade. We already knew what cars he had, but it led into my next question, which was what car was he driving the night Victoria was murdered. He said the Escalade because it had four-wheel drive. We believed him as he lives in Somerset on a high hill. You can see most of Somerset's western side from Seattle, which is quite a way away. Especially if you are in a tall building. He added he has been married to Mrs. Wilde for twenty years. He volunteered that he had two teenage boys. That ended his answers.

He wouldn't confide in the extramarital relations. I told him that it didn't matter whether he was faithful or not because I could get that info from Ruby, Sally, Jane, Rita, and several more but not from Victoria. He seemed to wilt a little at that point. He knew very well where my information came from, and he glanced in that direction. I didn't feel good about him knowing where the information came from. I knew Little Miss Receptionist could possibly be looking for another job soon. Well, it might be good for her to start living her life instead of watching it go by from the sidelines.

I asked how long he had been intimate with Victoria. He didn't want to lie, but to answer the question would make him, in his mind, a suspect. Mike just looked at him and started to get up. Mr. Wilde quickly said that he started to sleep with her about two and a half years ago right after she entered nursing school. But they hadn't been involved for a couple of months. She wasn't cooperative at first or thrilled about having to sleep with him. After they had done it a couple of times, she demanded money. She told him she would go to Mrs. Wilde and spill the beans if he didn't pay. He said she gave him a schedule of when and where they could get together and how much it would cost. I asked where these so-called meetings took place. He said usually they met at a cheap motel on Highway 99 or at her apartment.

I asked what he meant by cooperative. She said no when he first asked. But he told her if she wanted to continue working, she would have to do this favor for him. He knew she needed the money for school, so he was pretty sure she would do what he wanted. I asked if he was aware of the punishment for bribery. He held his head down and said no very softly.

I couldn't help feeling there was more to this, but at this point, I let it go. I asked if he had seen Victoria with anyone else around the company other than employees or her fiancée. He thought for a moment and then it was like a light came on. He said shortly before she started asking for money there was a man he didn't know hanging around the company. We asked if he had a chance to see what kind of car he drove. He couldn't see it as his office was in the back. He stated he had no way of seeing the street or parking lot.

Mike asked him if we brought in a sketch artist could he describe the man well enough for her to draw him. He said he couldn't but he knew the receptionist could give us a very good description. He caught her staring at him and told her to get back to work. Our last question was, do you know if other employees could give us any information about this man? He said he saw him talking with Rita. Right after that, she started asking for money. Mike asked him to bring her in so we could question her.

CHAPTER THREE

....

The Mystery Man and Rita

A FEW MINUTES LATER, a bewildered Mr. Wilde came in. No one has seen Rita today. It isn't like her; she is always on time. Even the day of the storm she arrived early. I asked for her address. We were told again to see Ms. Hastings to get that information. He added he didn't keep track of silly details. Mike told him not to leave the country as we might need to talk with him again. This comment was just to put the fear of God in him. Mike didn't like him either.

Mike and I left to see Ms. Hasting. We need to find out where Ms. Rita lives. The address Ms. Hastings gave us was in the Magnolia district up on the bluff. The bluff overlooks Puget Sound and has some very expensive homes.

When we got to her house, I was wondering what Rita actually did for TWC. It must be a very high-paying job. It couldn't be just a saleslady position. Her house is located in the ritziest part of Magnolia. It was extremely nice, and from the outside, it looked like it would be valued in the million-dollars-plus range. Also, the view from her house was to die for. It was something I would never be able to afford but could dream of. I saw Mike looking at it and trying to figure out the same thing.

"How did she buy this place?" I said.

Mike replied, "Your guess is as good as mine."

We rang the bell and waited a few minutes. When there was no answer, Mike decided to walk around the house to see if there was something amiss. We were concerned as there were no tire tracks from the garage to the street on the snow-covered driveway. That meant she had to have been home before the last snowfall and when Victoria was murdered.

I rang the bell again. A neighbor came out and shouted at me. She wanted to know what we were doing prowling around Ms. Rawlins' house and if we didn't leave she would call the police. I shouted back we are the police and Mrs. Rawlins's work reported her absent, which was highly suspicious. The neighbor then walked slowly over and said that she hadn't seen Rita since yesterday morning. She saw her leave for work and had commented that she thought it was too dangerous to be driving around in her expensive sports car. She said Rita responded back that she would be just fine and gave a hearty laugh and drove off.

I asked what kind of sports car did she drive. The neighbor said she wasn't sure. But it was a red foreign job her boyfriend gave her. Bingo, an expensive foreign car comes into the picture. Mike appeared at that time and reported that everything looked secure. We asked the neighbor if she by any chance had a key. She looked at us suspiciously. Both Mike and I took out our badges and ID to show her we were in fact police officers. We told her we could get a search warrant, but if Rita was in there hurt, it would take extra time. That got her hurrying over to her house as fast as the snow would let her go. She wasn't gone long before she brought back the front door key.

We told her she could come in with us but needed to stay behind us in case something happened. As we were entering the house, I asked her if she knew anything about Rita that might help us. She was eager to help. She told me that Rita had been married, but her husband was killed in an airplane crash. The life insurance settlement had been very generous, and the mortgage insurance had paid off the house. She said Rita could live quite comfortably for the rest of her life without even bothering to work.

I asked, "When did the accident happen?" After thinking a minute, she said it was about a year ago. I thought it strange that Rita already had a boyfriend. I asked the neighbor if she knew the boyfriend's name or how to get a hold of him. I had to explain he might know where Rita is. She didn't know his name or where he lived.

I asked if she could describe him. She said he was nice-looking, above-average height, but not real tall and had dark hair. That description sounded very familiar. She added he drove a dark blue Corvette. She wasn't sure of the year, but it was pretty new. Well, how many midnight-blue Corvettes could there be in the Seattle area anyway. Probably more than a hundred at least.

The house was elegantly appointed. We didn't find anything out of the ordinary without getting a search warrant. That would be our next step if Rita didn't turn up soon. We found a picture of her, which we took for an AP bulletin just in case we didn't find her soon. The neighbor was looking at us with a stern look on her face. We told the her why we took it and that it would be returned. We thanked her for being so helpful. We made sure the house was properly locked up. We got her name, and we gave her our cards. She said she would call us if Rita came home. With that, we left.

We headed back to TWC to question the receptionist, as we didn't have time to question her before we hurried off to Rita's house. We wanted to know if she could describe the man Rita knew. Luckily for us, she hadn't been canned and was still there.

We asked her if she ever saw Rita's mystery man. She had indeed, she said. She described him as about 5'10" tall, good-looking with dark hair. Sounded just like the description Rita's neighbor gave us. I asked if she noticed what kind of car he drove, but she said from her vantage point she couldn't see it. We asked if she saw him talking with any of the other ladies of the firm. She thought for a minute and gave us Victoria, Ruby Sally, Jane, and Rita. I hoped that she didn't put two and two together and remember these were the employee names she gave me before. The women who had "vibes" for the boss. Yuck!

We asked her to call Mr. Wilde and have him meet us in the conference room. We added, "Please call Ruby, Sally, and Jane and have them join us too." The receptionist almost titillated while dialing Mr. Wilde and the others.

We went to the conference room without waiting for the others. Once there, we talked about our strategy for questioning. We wanted this done before everyone arrived. Both of us knew we had to move quickly; otherwise, we might have more homicides to solve.

When everyone was seated, we went over the facts we had gathered and I wrote them on the whiteboard:

1. We knew they all had been sleeping with Mr. Wilde.
2. Rita's boyfriend had been in contact with all of them, including Victoria.
3. Victoria was murdered.
4. Rita was missing.
5. One set of tire track impressions taken at the murder scene were those of an expensive sports car.

Mike said, "You all need to tell us what is going on." I added, "Who wants to start talking first?" Mr. Wilde was silent. Sally started to cry. Ruby glared at her and Jane started to talk. She said Moe is the only name she ever heard Rita call her boyfriend.

"Rita told me she told Moe about Mr. Wilde making all of us sleep with him. He told her he had a plan that might work in our favor. Then Rita got us all together with Moe, and he laid out his plan to make Mr. Wilde pay for making us provide sexual favors." They were all mad and wanted revenge. So it made sense to them to do it.

"After we started asking for money, Moe came back and threatened to turn us over to the police. He told us we were involved in prostitution, which was illegal. He said he wouldn't contact the police if we gave him a percentage of the money we received from Mr. Wilde. He then told us his cut would be 50 percent, which was outrageous, but we didn't see a way out."

I asked how Rita felt about him charging them the large percentage rate. Ruby spoke up. She said Rita introduced them to Moe as someone who could help them out of their situation. So when he demanded the money from them, Rita didn't say much. It made me think she was in on it from the beginning.

Ruby continued, "Earlier, Rita told me her husband died in an accident, and she mentioned she got a large settlement after his death from the insurance company. Ruby was suspicious that Rita had done away with him for the insurance money. She was even more sure after Rita introduced Moe as her boyfriend. He was the kind you would hire to do a job not have as a boyfriend."

I said, "I don't understand about Rita having Moe kill her husband. I heard he died in an airplane crash."

Ruby said Rita confided in her that it was husband number two who was killed in the airplane accident. She remembered Rita saying the first one died in a car crash.

Ruby kept on talking. Moe wasn't really Rita's type, and she didn't act like she wanted him around. Her next comment was Rita married for money, style, and prestige. Moe might have the money, but he didn't have the other two qualities. He had nice looks but that wasn't what attracted Rita. She finished by saying on top of all that, Moe was sleazy.

My head was really starting to hurt. I think we just opened up the proverbial can of worms. One case was hard enough to solve, but now it looked like we had four all rolled into one. Victoria's murder, husbands one and two killed in so-called accidents, and now Rita was missing. I looked at Mike, and he was staring at the conference room table. I knew he was thinking the same thing.

Mike looked up and asked them if Victoria had tried to get some of her money back from Moe or had threatened to expose him. This time, Sally spoke up. She said she overheard Victoria talking on the phone with someone who she thought was Moe. "I heard her say she wasn't giving him any more money and wanted back what she had already given him. She also said she wouldn't solicit any more men, and she wouldn't sleep with any of his associates. She was engaged and wanted out."

That was all I heard of the conversation because my phone rang, and I had to leave to answer it. When I got back, Mike filled me in on what was said while I was gone. He said he asked Sally, "Did you say their associates?" She said, "Yes, that is what she heard her say."

I was up to speed, so I asked her to continue. She said, "I thought it strange about the associates, but at that moment I got a call about an order. When I hung up, I forgot to ask Victoria about her call."

I asked, "When did that call happen?"

She said it happened the day before Victoria was murdered. She lamented, "I should have stayed that night to help her get out the orders, but Rita told me she would help."

I looked at Mr. Wilde and said, "I thought you and Victoria were the only ones working and you left before she did?"

"Yes, that is what I said," he replied.

Sally spoke up, "No, I'm sure Rita told her she would help."

Again, Mr. Wilde said that he didn't see anyone else in the office except Victoria before he left. I asked, "Could Rita have gone and then returned?" Both Mr. Wilde and Sally said yes at the same time.

"We all have keys to the building," Jane said.

"What kind of foreign sports car does Rita drive?" asked Mike.

Ruby replied, "A new red Ferrari with the license plate MyRDash." My mind started to wander. I'm sure it stood for my red fast sports car. I bet she would go fast to draw a lot of attention. Get back on the topic, I told myself.

I looked at Mike and said we needed to check on what tires Ferrari is putting on their cars this year. Maybe they will match one of the impressions we got from the crime scene. With that, we wrapped up the interviews and told everyone to go someplace safe tonight and left.

When Mike and I got back to the station, we put out a BOLO on the red Ferrari with the plate MyRDash. It shouldn't be too hard to find. Unless, God forbid, it was at the bottom of Puget Sound. Huge cruise ships, container ships, ferries, fishing vessels, and all sorts of sports vessels travel Puget Sound. It is one of the deepest natural sounds in the United States. Some areas are hundreds of fathoms deep. It would take an eternity to find a car there.

Jim was in his office, and we entered unannounced. Normally, he asked for his officers to come in, but we couldn't wait. There was too much to tell him about the case. I was really glad he was seated and not elbow-deep in paperwork. Mike started with what we found out. I couldn't wait and broke into his conversation with, "And now it is four cases, maybe more."

Jim sat up straight and demanded to know why is it four cases. I told him Mr. Wilde had been sleeping with five of the woman at TWC. Mike told him how Rita was the one who introduce them to Moe. Moe suggested the ladies charge Mr. Wilde for their services. After they started to charge him, Moe told them they were now considered prostitutes by taking money for their acts. He said that he wouldn't say anything if they gave him 50 percent of the money they were getting. They all got scared and caved in to the blackmail.

We told him Ruby's suspicion about Rita having her two husbands murdered for their insurance money. Also, that she was sure Moe probably was the one who set up the airplane and car crashes. We added, "Ruby told us Moe didn't fit the description of what Rita looked for in husband material. She liked them to have money, style, and prestige. Moe didn't fit all of Rita's wants. On top of that, she told us he was, in her exact words, sleazy."

I started telling him about what Sally told us, that she overheard Victoria telling someone she wanted to get out of sleeping with his associates. "Per Mr. Wilde, she hadn't slept with him for a couple of months. So, I think Moe got her into servicing his associates to earn the extra 50 percent bribe. Sally also heard her say she was engaged now and didn't want to do this any longer. She said she wanted to get her money back. She didn't hear the whole conversation as she got a call regarding an order she had to take. That was the day before the murder. She also overheard Rita volunteering to stay late to help Victoria get the orders out otherwise Sally would have stayed.

"Mr. Wilde confirmed there was no one with Victoria when he left at 7:15 that evening. We asked around the office to find out what time Rita was last seen, and they all confirmed it was about 5:15 p.m. That means she had to return after Mr. Wilde left. The reason we believe this is because Rita drives a red Ferrari. It is new and probably matches the tire tread impression the techs took at the lot."

Jim sat there trying to absorb all the info we just gave him. As he was processing what we told him, my mind started to wander. What if Rita and Moe came back to TWC at the same time, did Rita go in to help Victoria while scheming on how to get her out without raising any suspicion? Or maybe there was a plan already in place. The plan could have been to have Victoria walk out with her as Moe waited by the backdoor. Okay, maybe Rita didn't know what Moe had planned until the jerk knocked Victoria out.

My mind was running wild once again. I hadn't been paying attention and finally noticed the office had become quiet. I looked up to see both Jim and Mike staring at me. Jim, being his nice self, asked me what had I been mulling over.

I told them what I was considering. Although I wasn't sure how they would like it. At times, my brain goes way out on a limb. To my amazement, they seemed pleased with my ideas. "We need all the angles we can come up with," Jim said. Keep thinking outside the box while you keep everything in perspective.

I said we need to know who this Moe guy really is and who his associates are. Mike and Jim spoke almost simultaneously; they were thinking the same thing. I was on a roll and contributing ideas that were worthwhile.

Jim said we need Moe's exact name. Mike and I already knew that. Mike suggested once we accomplish getting Moe's identity, we can see if he has a record. Maybe we would get lucky, and he has done something similar in other cities. Too bad there wasn't some sort of interstate reporting system. I said, "Don't forget we also need to check into the two deaths of Rita's husbands." Jim broke in and said he would get other detectives investigating that aspect of the case. Mike and I breathed a silent hallelujah!

Jim said, "Before you start checking on Moe's identity, you needed to check with Ben first to see if the DNA results are back. He did tell us he was going to put a rush on it."

Yeah, it has been a while since the tissues went to the lab, I thought. Mike and I headed back to our desks to call Ben. He told us he had just came back on shift after his day of sleep. He said he was exhausted and took a little extra time. That explained why we hadn't heard. Ben told us he would find the results and get back to us.

It was only a couple of minutes later when Mike's phone rang. It was Ben, so Mike put him on speaker. Jim came out of his office to listen with us. Ben told us the DNA belongs to a David Morella. He had been arrested before for a rape. That is why they had the DNA. Unlucky for us, he said the woman dropped the charges.

This was a huge break. Moe was probably a nickname for Morella. We could have DMV run through their records to find the make and model of his car or cars. They will also have his address. Now that we have his full name, we can check our records to see if he had been arrested for any other crime in the state.

His DNA was a nail in his coffin. I suggested we get a warrant for his bank records. The ladies should be able to give us the amount of money they gave him. The bank records would show he had deposited that amount of money. That would nail down the blackmail angle. Finally, we were on a solid roll.

It was still bothering me that nobody had seen Rita since the night of the murder. Nothing had come back on the BOLO for her car. It isn't hard to spot a red Ferrari. They are a dime a dozen. One thing we hadn't asked the Human Resources person for is Rita's cell number. Everyone has one now days. We called TWC and asked for Ms. Hastings so she could look up her cell number. She gave us 206-222-5555. She also gave us the carrier's name.

Since her neighbor told us Rita's last name was Rawlins, we had all the info we needed to call Verizon. We wanted to see if her cell had GPS. If it did and it hadn't been disabled, we could track down the location of the car. Mike called Verizon and identified himself as Detective Mike Bowers. He gave the person who answered at Verizon Rita Rawlins's name and cell number and asked whether it had GPS or another tracking program. The operator was quite nasty and told him that information was not given out. Mike said, "If we came in with a warrant, would the info be available?" The operator was not quite so snotty but still insisted we needed to come in person. We were mad that we had to jump through hoops when someone's life might be in jeopardy.

A call was put into Judge Hargrove, and he agreed to issue the warrant. We got to Verizon's office right before closing and were met with further hostility. "You might have come at a more convenient time" were the first words out of the receptionist's mouth. I said, "If you would have been more corporative, we wouldn't even be here." Mike produced the warrant and said he didn't care how much time it would take. We would wait for the information. A life might depend on what program was on Rita's cell. Finally, the idiot's brain came to life, and she scurried off to check Rita's contract. She came back and said the cell has GPS. Now we can get our techs on tracking it if the cell phone is still working.

Our techs are really good, and it wasn't long before they gave us a location. It wasn't a good one, and we feared she was another victim. The GPS was indicating the cell was at a park in North Seattle. It was Carkeek Park, and it is located between Third Avenue and Puget Sound. You need to drive to the Greenwood district and go North on Third Ave to 110th. You turn left off of Third and drive down a big hill into the parking lot. The park is secluded, hilly, wooded, and big. Amtrak and the Sounder Commuter train runs along the west side of the park. The train tracks are between some of the beach and the park. You need to cross a walkway above the tracks to access the water. So no one would see anything happening from either passing train.

We need a search party out there as quickly as possible. The park is too big for just a couple of officers. We put out the call for anyone in the vicinity to start a search. One officer called in to say he was near the park and volunteered to do a quick check of the lot.

At 6:12 p.m., he called to say he found the car without anyone inside. He asked if he could use a jimmy bar to open the car. Jim gave him the go-ahead. A request was in place for a canine unit to join the search party. The officers searching would need all the help they could get. With any luck, the dogs might catch Rita's scent from items left in her car.

Our luck was holding out as the snow hadn't returned, but it was getting dirty and a little slushy. The slush might have degraded the scent. We kept our fingers crossed that wouldn't be the case. Mike and I drove out to see if we could help. The search was well underway when we got there. We got out of the car and heard some shouting. We started running toward the shouts.

They found Rita, but she was in serious condition and barely alive. When we got to her, there were officers on their hands and knees gently pushing snow away from her. Others had run back to get blankets and emergency kits. Those items are standard in patrol cars. They were putting the blankets on and around her. An ambulance had already been called for. The officers not aiding Rita were collecting as much evidence as possible. It was so dark because of the time and all the trees around her that police were using flashlights to see what was there. Flashlights were the only light source available in this area of the park. We heard the ambulance siren in the distance, so we made a makeshift sling out of some blankets that were not being used. We didn't want to move her, but time was of the essence. We started heading down the hill and met the medics halfway there. They took over and hustled Rita into the ambulance.

After a brief look at her, the medics knew to take her directly to Harborview. There was no other hospital that would be able to save her. The medics alerted the ER. Nurses and doctors were waiting when the ambulance pulled in. Mike and I were right behind them.

Dr. Janice Richter was working the ER that night. She is a very competent doc. She quickly did the triage and called the surgery unit. "There is no time to waste," she told them. Dr. Richter added, "She is too critical to remain in the ER a minute longer."

They rushed Rita up to surgery. Dr. Richter didn't give us much hope. She did say the surgeons on duty at this time were the best and would do everything possible to save her. Now it was up to God. I agreed and said a lot of small prayers in my mind. We needed all the help we could get.

I asked if they would notify us when she was out of surgery. We both knew there was no way we could see her tonight but just knowing that she made it through would ease our minds. We conveyed that to Dr. Richter. She said that could be arranged. I was glad I had a lot of my business cards with me to give out, but they were running low. I left one with her, and we went back out to the car.

We drug our tired bodies back to the station. All the evidence had been turned in; Rita's car was impounded. It would be gone over with a fine-tooth comb. I told Mike before we leave I want to call the remaining ladies at TWC and make sure they are someplace safe. I got a hold of all them using the cell phone numbers they had given us. I breathed a sigh of relief. I reminded them to get someplace safe. Don't go home. I asked them to call if us right away if they needed help.

Mr. Wilde could fend for himself, but then I thought of Mrs. Wilde and their boys. They should be protected. I called and Mrs. Wilde answered. I told her to make sure their home was locked up tight and everyone was safe. She asked why, and I told her we found Rita beaten to a pulp and she was just barely alive. We are calling all the people at TWC warning them to do this as a precaution. She told me she was concerned as Mr. Wilde wasn't home yet. It was almost 8:45 p.m. At that moment, I heard the door open in the background, and he called out that he was home. Too bad! Why he rubbed me the wrong way was beyond me.

The one person I didn't know how to contact was the nosey miss receptionist. I didn't know her and didn't have a cell phone number for her. It was after closing, so I couldn't call Ms. Hastings. We had to hope she wasn't part of Moe's plan to get rid of all the witnesses. If that was indeed his plan. Mike and I sat at our desks in silence for a while gathering strength to get up and go home.

About an hour later, we felt like we were ready to leave when a call came in from Harborview. Dr. Richter told us Rita was out of surgery and in ICU. She added some of the injuries weren't addressed because she isn't in the best shape to handle more anesthesia. They stabilized her, and she would be kept in a coma for now. There are more surgeries scheduled for the near future.

I asked Dr. Richter if there was a guard on duty in the ICU. I didn't want Moe or his associate to get wind that she isn't dead. I was assured Rita would have someone nearby at all times. I hope the news people haven't gotten wind of a person barely alive was found in Carkeek Park.

There usually were reporters camped out in front of Harborview. They already had a blurb in the papers about Victoria's murder. How they got that news was beyond us.

CHAPTER FOUR

....

One Found, There's Moe to Go! What About Andy?

I WAS REALLY BEGINNING to miss my apartment. There have been too many long days working this homicide. It was only a little over forty-eight hours, but it felt like a whole week had gone by. Right now, my focus was on what was there to eat when I get home. We said good night and went our separate ways.

I was home at last. After surveying the kitchen for the second night in a row, I knew I really needed to go to the store. The refrigerator and cupboards were almost bare. Nothing in the refrigerator except condiments, a lone tomato, and a jar of pickles. Well, at least there was a package of sausages and some buns in the freezer. Into the microwave they went. I'll add some pickles and a tomato slice or two for my vegetable and fruit—voilà dinner is served. I wish I had some onions to add but no such luck—not for healthy a dinner but something to ease my hunger pangs.

With my stomach full, I knew I needed a quick shower. The water was hot, which was pleasing to me. Wow, now I almost feel human. If only my brain will stop going in twenty different directions and let me sleep. My bed feels so good. Now I pray, please let me fall asleep fast.

Tossing and turning, I feel like a spinning top. Darn, so much for sleep happening. I wish I could learn to turn off my mega information system. After another hour, I give up on sleep. I go to the kitchen table and start writing down details regarding this case. I'm most concerned on how are we going to track down Moe. We have his address, but will he be foolish enough to still be there? After a while, I tell myself we will be able to make some progress tomorrow. I drag myself to the bedroom. In bed once again and for the one hundredth time, I tell myself go to sleep over and over again.

How did it get to be 6:00 a.m. so fast? Wash, dress, breakfast, and I'm out the door. Wait, first don't I need to get out of bed. My stomach was yelling at me: yes, you must eat. I considered what there was left to eat, and voilà, I'll have some Honey Nut Cheerios sans the milk, darn. Add some coffee and maybe include some toast coated with butter cinnamon and sugar. That thought got me going. I was just finishing cleaning up the kitchen when there was a knock at my door.

Who in the world is visiting so early? When I opened the door, Mike was standing there with a glum look on his face. I said, "Come in and give me the not-so-good news." There was coffee left, so I poured him a cup before he had a chance to ask. I told him to sit down and talk. Before he said anything about what was going on, he scolded me for not asking who was on the other side of the door before opening it. "Yah, yah," I said.

With that said and done, he started explaining about the other day when he was late getting to TWC. He had to stop at the hospital. His dad was there and wasn't doing well. He went by last night and sat with him for a while and he seemed okay. He said they had a good chat, and he told his dad he would be back in the morning. He said he gave him a kiss on the forehead and left.

Most men don't show that much affection for their dads, but Mike really loved his. He went on to say early this morning the hospital call to let him know his dad had passed. I felt terrible. I got up and gave him a big hug. I said if he needed anything just ask. He said that right now all he needed was to get the bastard that was causing all this havoc. He would have been at the hospital when his dad passed if it weren't for this damn case.

He stopped for a second and took a deep breath and caught the tears before they fell. He started to talk again. His dad told him what he wanted done in case he didn't make it this time. Mike said he gave the hospital and mortuary the instructions of what his dad's wishes were. The mortuary agreed they would cremate him and hold his ashes until this case was solved. All of his dad's friends were gone, so Mr. Bowers asked Mike not to bother having a funeral. He was the only family he had left, so it didn't make sense for him to waste a bunch of money. Mike said his dad's exact words were, "You will be the only one there except the pastor, and I don't want you to waste the money." Mike didn't care about the money, but he loved his dad and wanted to honor his wishes. Mike would lay him to rest beside his mother when the time was right.

I asked him if it would be all right if I went with him to the cemetery. I met his dad several times at the station when he came by to spend time with Mike. Mr. Bowers was such a nice man, and we hit it off right away. Mike knew his dad liked me. He stood up and said he wouldn't have it any other way.

I knew I needed to get Mike's mind off his dad, so I suggested we go directly to Moe's place. Mike smiled a little and said, "You really know how to cheer a guy up." I gently slapped him on his shoulder and said, "Knock it off. Let's get going." We got in my car. I didn't want Mike's mind wandering while driving. He called the station and told them we were headed to Moe's place. We will call if backup is necessary.

The place was really nice but not spectacular. His apartment or should I say condo was in the old Queen Anne High School. The school had been renovated and made into condos years before. We knocked waited, and there was no response. We listened and no sound was coming from inside. As I suspected, Moe wasn't there. We located the condo manager and asked if we could have a look in his unit. Of course, he said not without a warrant. We asked him when he last saw Moe. He did reply to this and said he thought it was a couple of days ago. I asked if he had seen anyone with him. No again.

"Did Moe have any visitors?" Bingo! The right question. When Mike asked that, he started talking. There was a stream of people coming and going all the time. Mike asked if he knew any of their names or could describe them. He said he didn't know them by name, but he could describe some of them. We asked if he wouldn't mind coming with us to the station to give our sketch artist details of what they looked like. He said he would come, just give him a second to lock up his unit. He met us at the curb and off we went.

When we arrived at the station, Mike took the condo manager to Shelly's office. She is a great sketch artist and could even get a blind person to describe someone. It was a talent I didn't have and envied it.

While I was waiting for Mike, Jim came out to see if we had any information on Rita's condition. I said I hadn't heard from the hospital yet. As a matter of fact, we haven't heard from any of the women. I am a little worried because we don't know how far Moe and his associates will go to remain free. He knows he has a target on his back and we are looking for him. No telling what he will do.

Jim said not to worry about the ladies as they were told to go someplace safe. I'm sure that is exactly what they did. I smiled and said thanks.

In a short while, Mike came back carrying two sketches. He said, "Do you want the good news first or the good news?" I punched Mike in the arm and said, "Don't be a smart-ass." I guess I came across a little too grouchy? Jim just looked at us shook his head and headed into his office. He knew we were tense and needed space from him for a while.

Mike showed me Shelly's sketches. One was of Andy, the other was Mr. Wilde. He said after Shelly finished the sketches, she let the condo manager look at them. I told him to look carefully at them as they were suspects in a murder that happened yesterday. The manager said Mr. Wilde came by earlier the day before and Andy came by that evening. I gasped. He called Andy and Mr. Wilde by name. Mike smiled. After that slipped out, the manager said he had forgotten their names until he saw the sketches, and he sure as hell didn't want to get involved in a murder investigation. He volunteered that both had been to Moe's condo several times.

Mike said, "Shelly is working on sketches of other visitors. She will bring them to us when they are complete."

I was wondering what their connection was. "This doesn't make sense," I said.

Mike shrugged his shoulders. He said, "We will be able to put it all together when the pieces fall into place."

We headed into Jim's office and updated him on who the sketches were. I asked Mike if a sketch of Moe was being done. We need to circulate it throughout the area. Mike headed back to Shelly's office to make sure the condo manager gave her a description of Moe.

I drove with Mike back to Moe's place, but this time with a key. The condo manager had a master for all the units, which he gave us. He didn't want to be a conspirator in a murder.

We received the search warrant and had it in hand. We went through the rooms one at a time. We didn't want to miss anything. Searching the bedroom, we found blood on the sheets. We were hoping more than one type would be on them. Like Moe's along with Victoria's. Scratches tend to bleed, so there was a good possibility some of the blood was his. We bagged the sheets carefully. We didn't want to contaminate them accidently. Nothing needed to be included other than the DNA we wanted.

I believe Victoria was smart in scratching her assailant. Or maybe she was just fighting him off. Either way, it was helping us. We both had an idea she knew she wouldn't live through what was happening to her. I feel deep down that she was leading us to her killer through the DNA.

If the DNA tests came back the way we hoped, we would have two ways of identifying her murderer. Prosecutors loved a slam dunk and two important incriminating pieces of evidence could do it. Now if the murder weapon was here… We tore the rest of the condo apart. There was so much junk and filth around that it was hard to go through it. We didn't find the murder weapon, but we had plenty of other items that could include evidence.

"What a pigpen Moe's condo is," I said. I feel like I need a penicillin shot and a scalding hot shower so I won't come down with anything. Mike agreed and said he wanted a quick shower too. He added, "That was disturbingly disgusting."

When we were out in the fresh air, I could finally take a deep breath. Mike was doing exactly the same thing. I said, "I didn't know a place could smell and look that bad." Mike agreed. He was putting on some hand cleaner and told me to put out my hands so he could give me some. I gladly did as he asked.

We already had the evidence in the trunk because of the smell. I drove back as quickly as possible to the lab. We felt sorry for the techs because everything was soiled and smelled really bad. There were sheets with hairs and blood on them. Some of the hairs had follicles attached. We collected cigarette butts along with dirty cups and glasses with fingerprints on them, including some possible DNA.

We collected an assortment of papers we found in piles that look like they might be important. We didn't have time to go through all of them, but there could be some information in them. They hoped they would also provide fingerprints of some of his associates. The lab techs probably wouldn't need to go over the loose change, theater tickets, and miscellaneous junk; but we included it all.

We headed up to the squad room. Since Andy was a frequent visitor at Moe's, I called Duncan to see if Andy was there. We wanted to ask him more questions. Duncan said he came home after seeing the Clumps but went directly to his room without so much as a hello. "He left yesterday while I was working and he hasn't come back yet." I asked if Andy had visitors over to the apartment. He said his phone rang often, but no one came by but Victoria. I thanked him and hung up. What was Andy up to, and where was he?

We called the Clumps to see if they had any contact with Andy since we were at their home. They hadn't seen him since that night. They added they were sure he was studying for his finals. I asked if they knew of any place he might be. They remembered Victoria telling them he had a trailer for camping. It was stored in a lot in Lynnwood near the freeway. They said Victoria told them he had a friend who had a cabin on an island. He would take the trailer up there sometimes to get away.

"Did she happen to mention what island it was?" we asked.

They thought it was Camano Island. We thanked them for the information and said goodbye.

When we got off the phone, we immediately got on our computers searching for the storage lot's location. I found one in Lynnwood, and it was next to the freeway like the Clumps said. It had to be the one. It looked like it would be a little difficult to get to, so just in case, I printed off the directions. We headed out to get another warrant. We didn't want to turn around in case we needed it.

The warrant didn't take long to get to us. So with it in hand, off we went. I asked Mike on the way, "How many miles do you think we have racked up so far?"

He said he hadn't had time to even guess. "Too many I'm sure," he intoned while winding his way through the traffic. Lynnwood is about nineteen miles from Seattle, but the traffic can be a bear at certain times of the day.

When we got there, we found the attendant right away. We showed him the search warrant. He was able to give us the trailer location and gave us a key. He said they always requested a key in case there was a fire or any other catastrophe.

We had no trouble finding the trailer and started our search. It wasn't very big, so it was easy to go through. The items we were hoping to find there were Victoria's fingernails and the boot. No such luck. We did find blood and swabbed the area for DNA. It was in a sink, so it could be from a cooking accident, but we collected it anyway. We found fingerprints, which we dusted and collected. There were dirty dishes on the counters, but they looked like they had been there longer than the time frame we needed.

"Do guys always live like pigs, or is it just these two?" I asked. "Yuck," I said.

Mike replied, "Only scumbags live like pigs."

We decided to look around the outside of the trailer in case something was dropped without anyone noticing it. What we found was a dark blue Corvette parked on the far side of the trailer. What a coincidence. We hadn't come looking for it; it just fell into our laps. Thank you, God!

We went back to the lot's office and asked about the Corvette. The attendant said that it belonged to a guy called Moe. He left it here when he picked up the Jeep that was stored here. He told us Moe and Andy came in together, and Moe told him he wanted to drive up to his cabin yesterday. He said they jumped into the Jeep and hightailed out of the lot. Moe was driving like a bat out of hell. In fact, he was driving like the devil was after him.

We told him some officers will be coming up to get the trailer and Corvette. We knew Jim would want the lab guys to go over them. We thanked him for his help and headed back to the station.

The search warrant didn't include the Corvette. We wanted to go through it, but we knew it would end up costing us in the end. If you find something, it wouldn't be admissible in court without a warrant. It would be classified as found in an unlawful search.

We headed back to the station. Jim was waiting to hear what we found. We told him about finding the trailer plus the Corvette. We said we found some bloodstains, which we swabbed, and other items. We dropped all of it off at the lab. The attendant also told us that Moe and Andy were there together yesterday. They picked up a Jeep that stored there. He added that they hightailed out of there like a bat out of hell. Moe was driving like the devil was after him, to quote the lot's attendant.

We surmised they were heading to the cabin. Jim said he has a friend, Bob Ferguson, who works for the Island County Police Department. He worked for the Seattle Police Department until he got a chance to move to the islands and into a new job. He is now a captain up there. "We keep in touch and have helped each other out over the years."

He went in his office to call him. He yelled at us to get a warrant and have the Corvette brought into the impound area while he was dialing Bob's number. He added, "The techs need to go over it thoroughly. Maybe they should bring in the trailer too."

"We already have the search warrant for it. There could be something that was overlooked or not visible to the naked eye."

Mike and I went down to the impound garage and told them where to get the trailer and Corvette. I handed them the directions

I had printed out. We said, "The lieutenant wants both gone over thoroughly as we might have missed something. He thinks there could be evidence not seen by the naked eye." I had already called from the squad room for a warrant before we headed downstairs. It arrived right away, and the trucks pulled out heading for Lynnwood.

"We need to get the license number of that Jeep," I said. Back in the squad room, we called the DMV and gave them the owner name and said it was a Jeep. Why we hadn't found it the first time we were getting the Corvette info was a mystery in itself. The DMV said there isn't a Jeep listed in Moe's name.

My brain kicked into gear and I said, "Look under Mr. Wilde or Andy Matthews's names." Bingo! It was listed under Andy's name as the owner. They gave us the plate number, color, year, and address it was registered at. This wasn't Andy's home address, it was Moe's. Why is the big question. What connection is there between Moe and Andy? I was thinking, where is Andy's SUV? It wasn't at Moe's place when we were searching the condo. I didn't have time to dwell on any of this. "We need another BOLO issued for the Jeep. Maybe on the SUV too," I added.

We wanted to talk with Mr. Wilde to see why he hadn't said he was so friendly with Moe. He downright lied to us. The manager of Moe's condo identified him as one of the friends often calling on him. As a matter of fact, on the very day Victoria was murdered. I called TWC and was told he wasn't there and hadn't been in all morning. I then called his home phone number. Mrs. Wilde answered. She told us he left for work at 7:20 that morning. I casually asked what car he was driving when he left. She said the Escalade as it was still snowy at their house. I didn't want to upset her, so I didn't tell her he never showed up to work.

Now we were looking for the Jeep, SUV, and the Escalade. My suspicions where they are at the same location. Again, I wondered what their connection was. Maybe Rita knew the answer, but as long as she was in a coma, we weren't going to get the answers from her. This is getting to be a mystery inside a mystery compounded by a mystery. I better quit going in that direction. My brain was on over-load again.

The impound guys were back with the Corvette and trailer. They were just unloading them off the trucks when Mike and I walked in. They all shouted at the same time, "We don't have any info yet." Well, duh! We just wanted to take a peek inside to see if there was a boot or fingernails laying in plain sight.

The guys popped the trunk, and there was the red boot. There was also a pool of dried blood, which we knew was Victoria's. The nails were there too. We left in a hurry and let them bag the evidence.

We went straight to Jim's office and told him to get a warrant for Moe's arrest. "You should probably add Mr. Wilde's and Andy's names as well." Jim asked if there was evidence to back up getting the warrants. We both said, "We have sufficient evidence." Mike and I shouted, "The boot and fingernails were in the trunk of the vet."

Jim smiled and said, "Well, okay then. I'll call Bob and give him this info."

CHAPTER FIVE

....

The San Juan Islands

CAPTAIN FERGUSON WAS IN, and Jim told him the men they were looking for were murder suspects. They were probably armed and suspected to be dangerous. The judge was in the process of issuing warrants for their arrests. Bob said they were still checking the county records to see if Duane Morella had property listed in his name. As soon as he had the location, he would call. Jim thanked him and hung up.

I wasn't in the mood to get a lot of dirty looks, but I suggested to Mike that we drive up there right now. Instead of the dirty look, he said, "Are you crazy?"

I said, "What if the Island County Police locate the cabin and don't call us until they find them? I want to be there if they do."

My mind was working in overtime again. If Moe knocked her out at the parking lot and shoved her in his trunk, he would have then driven her to his condo. There he did horrible things to her. The rape itself would have been terrible enough to have endured.

Then it was back in the trunk and off to TWC's lot to dump her body. That was when all the blood pooled in the trunk. Her fingernail might have come off when she tried to get out of the trunk, but she bled out too soon. Her boot probably came off when he was taking her out to place her by her car.

The attendant at the storage place couldn't see the trailer from the office. The lot is large with a lot of boats, trailers, and assorted vehicles. Or he was reading a book. I saw one on the desk. Since Moe's clothes weren't in his apartment, he could have gotten rid of them there. Or he probably buried them at the storage lot or has them at his cabin.

My thoughts were interrupted by Jim's voice coming loud and clear from his office. There was a message from an officer at the Island County Police department. He told us the cabin has been located, and some officers are on their way out there to set up a perimeter.

We hurried to Jim's office. He got on the phone right away to call Bob. The person answering said the captain wasn't in. He is on his way out to the cabin with the other officers. We asked that they stake out the cabin and wait for us to get there. The officer said he would contact the captain and give him the message. We drove really fast with sirens blazing and got to the site in less than fifty minutes.

We found Captain Ferguson at a vantage point above the cabin. We introduced ourselves. He told us to call him Captain Bob. He said some of his officers had spotted a Jeep and an Escalade. They saw a couple of guys going in and out. We asked if there was a way we could get close enough to take them by surprise. He said, "I have officers stationed to the south, some to the north, and us to the east." The cabin is situated on a cliff overlooking Puget Sound so there wasn't any egress to the west.

The cabin is surrounded. There isn't any way for them to escape. All we need to do is use the bullhorn and tell them to come out with their hands up. If there is unlawful action, a couple of well-placed shots should get their carcasses moving. We said, "Okay, if that's the plan, let's get moving."

Trying to get them to come out quietly didn't work. They took several wild shots from the front, side, and rear of the cabin. Responding shots rang out from all directions in answer to theirs. Like Captain Bob said, a few shots will have them running out of the cabin. First, their guns and rifles came flying through the air. Then they looked like rats scurrying from a sinking ship. They came out with their arms held high. That is, except for Mr. Wilde.

He took one round in his in shoulder, so he only had one arm raised. The officers closed in on them and took them without much trouble. Captain Bob said they would go over the cabin and vehicles very carefully. All evidence will be collected, catalogued, and sent back to Seattle when they were sure there wasn't anything else to be found.

An Island County officer rode along with Mr. Wilde as a guard in a medical helicopter to Harborview. Captain Bob said he would send a patrol car to pick him up. We thanked him for all his help and would wait probably impatiently to see what they found in the cabin. He chuckled and said, "No problem. Happy to be of service." He asked us to tell Jim he owed him and would collect, all the while smiling. I'm sure he would.

We got back with the two prisoners and took them to booking. They were the jailors' problem now. Then we headed to Jim's office. It was late, but we waited for the call from Bob. It was an hour and a half before the call came in. Captain Bob told us there wasn't much in the cabin except for Moe's bloody clothes. He tried to wash them in the kitchen sink without much luck. There were still spots of blood that hadn't come out. There were beer bottles and other assorted items. They bagged all the evidence and had a state trooper on the way to us.

Captain Bob said the most important item they found was a tire iron. It looked like there was dried blood on it. It was found in the Jeep that Andy owned but was actually Moe's.

Before Captain Bob hung up, Jim thanked him for all of us. He told him he was a godsend. If Bob hadn't acted as quickly as he did, we might never have found the evidence. Bob said, "No problem. Just remember you owe me," and chuckled. Jim said, "Will a fifth of good Bourbon that doesn't cost an arm and a leg do? If so, it is on its way." He smiled, said goodbye, and hung up.

I quietly said a small prayer of thanks to God. Without the freezing weather, the scumbags probably would have burned or buried all the evidence before we had a chance to apprehend them.

We have enough evidence to charge Moe with murder and hopefully the attempted murder of Rita. We have the murder weapon if it has Victoria's blood on it. The hopeful part is that Rita's blood is on it too.

Now we need to connect the other two scumbags, Andy and Mr. Wilde, to Victoria's brutal murder. Maybe they took part in Rita's horrendous beating too. Regardless either way, they won't be getting out soon. We have enough evidence to keep Moe for a long time. And enough on Mr. Wilde and Andy for shooting at officers and helping a murderer evade capture as well as them resisting arrest.

Jim asked, "Has anyone heard anything more from the hospital regarding Rita? Or for that matter the condition of Mr. Wilde?" As far as anyone knew, no one had reported in. He told me to call Officer Davis. Then he said, "We need to make contact with the other three ladies who were being blackmailed as well." Jim then asked Mike to get someone checking on them.

Officer Davis was sent to Harborview to guard Mr. Wilde after he was returned to his room from recovery. We didn't want to use Harborview's security as Mr. Wilde was a suspect in an ongoing murder case. Jeff told us he wasn't making any sense yet. The surgery had gone well, and he should be coherent within the hour. Mrs. Wilde was notified that her husband was being operated on at Harborview. She came and stayed until he was brought to his room. She left after seeing him and hearing he was going to survive. Jeff's opinion was, she would be contacting an attorney when she got home. She was mad as a wet hen and crying when she heard we found him at Moe's cabin. Before she left, she said she couldn't stand by a man who was associated with a killer. She had no idea he even associated with Moe, that lowlife.

I felt sorry for her and their two boys. The teen years are hard enough without having a criminal for a father. Kids at school or in the neighborhood can be so cruel.

I asked Jeff if he knew who was guarding Rita. He said it is a hospital security guard. "I know him personally and respect his abilities. You needn't worry about her at all." I thanked him and told him to call us when Mr. Wilde is coherent. He assured me he would. Jeff is a great officer. I had no worries that he wouldn't do exactly what he said.

Next, I called the ICU to check on Rita's progress. A nurse answered and said she was in surgery. The first one had been somewhat successful, and her condition was favorable for the next surgery. This one would take about three more hours. This was possibly the one that would save Rita's life. She told us it was a difficult surgery but not the last. I thanked her and asked, "If you are still on duty when she comes out of surgery, would you please call us to let us know how she is doing?" The nurse assured me she would either call or leave a message for the next nurse on duty to call us. I gave her the office number, mine and Mike's cell phone numbers, and thanked her again.

CHAPTER SIX

....

Trying to Sort Out the Connections

NOW THAT WE HAD all three in custody, I need to find Sally, Ruby, and Jane. We need to call the officer Mike put in charge of the search party. I want to make sure they are okay. We were also hoping they might have an idea why Mr. Wilde and Andy were in cahoots with Moe.

Mike and I went to TWC. We asked to see Ms. Hastings. The new receptionist called her office. She didn't answer the phone. We asked her to page her. She paged her and there was still no response. Now what in the world is going on? The receptionist looked at both of us and saw the disbelief and frustration. She thought for a moment and told us, "Ms. Hastings has an administrative assistant." She added when she started this position she was given a list of all employees and what they did. She explained Nancy supported both Mr. Wilde and Ms. Hastings. We asked her to have Nancy meet us in the conference room.

Nancy was a nice and quite competent older woman. We asked her if Ms. Hastings was coming in. Nancy said she hadn't heard from Sue, Ms. Hastings, today. She further explained if she wasn't coming in normally she would call to let her know. Mike asked her if there was an employee directory with addresses and phone numbers. "Of course," she said. She added she would be glad to give us a copy if we wanted it. Both of us answer with a resounding yes. Nancy left to get the directory and to make the copies. Mike looked at me and said, "I'm really getting an uneasy feeling. I think we need to get a warrant to search the whole business. It needs to cover the offices, the factory, and warehouse." I agreed. At that moment, Nancy came in with the copy of the directory. We thanked her and left.

What in the world is going on at that company? One woman killed, another in critical condition, and now a Human Resources person MIA. We could go over to her home or just forge on with getting the search warrant. We decided to go with getting the warrant.

We didn't go back to the office but headed directly to the King County Court House. We called Jim as we were on our way and asked him to arrange for the warrant. He agreed with our plan after we explained what had happened at TWC. He would call as soon as he hung up he said. We added make sure it is for the whole operation. He said okay!

I looked at Mike and said I hoped Hargrove is in. He really knows what we are up against. Mike nodded in agreement. We stopped in the lobby and asked for him. We were told he was in court but should be out momentarily. We told the bailiff we would wait and asked if he would let the judge know we were waiting.

The bailiff handed Hargrove the message. So when court was over, he headed our way. He said, "What is this warrant for?" We gave him a brief synopsis of what was going on. He got on his cell and was told by his assistant he had already drawn up the warrant to include the whole operation per the lieutenant's instruction. Judge Hargrove said he was happy his assistant was on top of everything and chuckled. "I think he needs a raise."

We didn't have to wait long for the assistant to bring the warrant down for Hargrove's signature. We called Jim and told him we were headed back to TWC with the warrant in hand. Jim said he thought this was getting too big. He wanted to call in the FBI. I quickly said, "Please don't do that. Give us a chance to see what we find." He reluctantly agreed. "Several officers will meet you there. This is going to be a big operation."

Mike looked at me and I explained what Jim wanted to do. Mike said, "Good girl. We don't want the FBI to get in the way yet."

We pulled up in front of TWC as a couple of cruisers headed into the parking lot. They placed themselves at the front of the parking lot entrance and at the back at the loading dock blocking any egress. Nothing would be going out of any door before we had a look at it. A couple of beat cops showed up along with several other officers.

We all entered the building. We asked the receptionist to get the person in charge while Mr. Wilde was away. She said, "It would normally be Ms. Hastings, but since she isn't here, I'll get Mr. Crane."

He came into the reception area. He told us he was in charge of the factory and warehouse portions of the company. He could accompany us anywhere in that area we wanted to see. From his demeanor, I was sure he had no idea anything was out of the ordinary. I asked who we would see to access the office area. He said we should call Sue as she was Mr. Wilde's right hand. Well, Sue wasn't here, so I guess Nancy will have to do.

While we were talking with Mr. Crane, our techs and forensic people started coming into the building. They requested to see the person in charge of the office area. We yelled, "Have the receptionist call Nancy." Several other officers followed close behind them. One of our forensic guys was very good at going over financial information. He was accompanied by a computer tech.

They would tackle that area of the company. Nancy was called to show them the way to accounting. She was also asked to give them access to Ms. Hastings's office. We told them to hold off on going through Mr. Wilde's office as we wanted to go over it.

We instructed the receptionist to have all employees stay in the building as we needed to talk with them. Then we all went in different directions to start our search. It wasn't long before employees began complaining and asking when we would be leaving. They said we were interrupting their work. We assured them we were working as quickly as possible and they would be able to return to work when we were done. We didn't add unless we find something fishy going on. Then each and every one of them would be questioned before they left.

Mike and I started searching the factory with Mr. Crane. It looked clean and neat with nothing out of order. I asked how the merchandise was stored and then shipped. He took us to the warehouse and shipping areas.

Mike saw some large locked cabinet doors along one side of the warehouse. He asked him about them. Mr. Crane said he didn't know what was behind those doors. Mr. Wilde had the keys and kept them locked except of course when he entered them. I asked if he ever saw anyone else accompanying him when he was in there. He thought for a second or two and said yes, there were several times when some other men were with him. We both asked at the same time, "What did the men look like?" Mr. Crane said he didn't pay much attention, but he thought one was older with black hair and about 5'10". The other was younger and nice-looking. He also had dark hair. Bingo! We have a connection, but what does it mean?

We asked if he was ever able to look into the cabinets. Mr. Crane said he was never permitted to watch them open the cabinets or go near them. He had to make himself scarce during business hours if Mr. Wilde was working in them. He didn't go in them very often while people were at work. We asked Mr. Crane to call Nancy and have her bring the keys down. He called and repeated our request. She said she wasn't sure where the keys were. Mike got on the phone and asked her to go through Mr. Wilde's desk. She said it was locked and she wasn't permitted to go through it. Mike said, "No problem. We will be there in a minute."

I asked Mr. Crane if there was a crowbar in the factory or something else we could use to pry open a locked desk.

He looked at us as if we had lost our minds. We explained we had a warrant that allowed us to search everything. He said, "Oh," and toddled off to the factory with us close behind. He gave us a long screwdriver, a crowbar, and a pry bar. "Will these work?" he asked.

"Those will do just fine," we replied.

We left him with a thank you and a blank look on his face. We got to Mr. Wilde's office. Nancy wasn't sure we should be breaking into his desk. We gave her the blurb that the warrant allowed us to search everything including locked doors, desks, and safes. We told her if she would rather not be present, it was okay for her to leave. She left.

Mike went to the desk and started jimmying the drawers. I started looking through file cabinets and wondered where the safe was. The third file drawer was labeled J through L. The keys couldn't possibly be in this file cabinet. Doesn't key start with a K? How silly would that be. At the back of the third file drawer, I found a locked box. It didn't look too sturdy, so I tried to pry it open with no luck. It was stronger than it looked. Now I knew it had to be something worth opening.

Mike had all the desk drawers opened by then and saw me struggling to open the box. He came over to give me a hand. It popped open on his first attempt. Darn, I'd tried three times with no results. Lo and behold, it contained a fountain of information. The keys were also in there and marked cabinet doors.

In there was a map with directions to something. We would look at it more after we got everything out. Letters were also in the box. Some of them were already written and addressed to Rita. So Mr. "Scumbag" Wilde was the one blackmailing Rita. I bet he got Moe to confess to the prostitution idea, and Moe used Rita's info about her two husbands as leverage. Or maybe he was the mastermind all along. We didn't speculate long as we wanted to see what was behind doors one, two, and three.

You would think something this important would be locked up. Then again, who would have thought to go through file cabinets? What's that saying about things hiding in plain sight. Well, we didn't believe in that scenario. Mike said there were some items in the desk, but we can go through those later. We were dying to see what was in those cabinets.

We hurried down to the warehouse. Jim appeared as we were heading there. We pulled him along and talked on the way. We were really excited to see what was so important it needed to be locked up. The suspense was killing me. I really have no patience for surprises. It was like waiting to open presents on Christmas morning. I wasn't good at waiting for that either. My parents never knew how impatient I was. Most presents were never a secret.

Finally, Mike inserted the first key. I was thinking, okay, I won't yank the door out of his hand and open it. I wanted to do that more than anything but for once controlled myself. Once we got a good look inside, we all stood there with our mouths open.

I said, "Can you believe there is that much cash just sitting in a large unprotected cabinet?"

Jim just said, "We need to get more officers down here to count it and bag it all up."

"It would be better if they filled file boxes with the money and take them to a bank where they have counting machines," I suggested.

Jim said, "Good idea, but for now, close and lock the cabinet back up."

Now for door two. It wasn't as joyous a discovery as the first one. It was full of drugs—marijuana, cocaine, and other drugs I didn't even know the names of. We left it open and opened the third door. It was a miniature office.

There was a desk, a couple of chairs, a computer, a file cabinet, and a small dusty wired window. I saw a light hanging above the desk and turn it on. It was much better now that we could see without squinting. We need access to that computer. It probably holds the names of people who buys them, not to mention the drug cartel names. Jim was on his cell already calling our computer tech. He told him in no uncertain terms to get his butt down to the warehouse now. All of us were sure the computer was password protected.

Jim asked Mike to call the DEA so they would come get the drugs off the property. We told them our tech was trying to access the computer. They said their computer tech would come to assist. He was used to breaking the passwords of drug cartels. Jim said, "Thank you. We need all the help we can get."

CHAPTER SEVEN

....

Made the Connection

HAVING MR. CRANE TELL us about the three scumbags working together in the warehouse cabinets, we now know how they are connected. I was thinking these lowlifes are dealing in drugs and making women give them sexual favors. I was thoroughly disgusted. Brain on overload once again. Get back on course, Amy.

I said, "Our next step should be to find out how everyone else fit into this scenario."

"Has anyone heard from the officers sent out to find the other three ladies?" Jim yelled. Everyone yelled back no, they hadn't heard a thing.

"I guess we can assume they are still in the wind," I said.

Jim started yelling out instructions. "We need to check the airport, train station, and bus lines to see if they left town. Ms. Hastings is another missing person we need to track down." He told Mike and me that we were done checking out TWC, the other officers here can wrap this up. "Get all the evidence back to the station and then find out how or where Ms. Hastings is."

On the way to the station, I was wondering why we hadn't searched Victoria's apartment. I was thinking we would maybe find something there. I said, "We haven't set foot in Victoria's apartment yet. Now is our chance. Let's get this stuff turned in and then go over there." We told the Clumps not to go to her apartment until we called and said it was okay. I was hoping they had done what we asked them to do.

We knew that Victoria lived in a small apartment on Capitol Hill. It wasn't far from downtown Seattle or Seattle University where she was taking her nursing courses. Her manager knew about her death and let us in. It didn't hurt that the Clumps told her we would be coming to check it out.

The apartment was neat and clean. She had a living room combined with her kitchen and eating area. There was a separate bedroom and bath. I took the bedroom, and Mike said he would check the rest. I yelled, "Leave the bathroom for me." I didn't want him to have to go through her personal feminine products. I started going through her one and only dresser. I found a packet of letters and put them in an evidence bag. In the closet was a box of files. They looked like they were from TWC. "I will definitely need a bigger evidence bag," I said to myself jokingly. That wasn't necessary as the box would be sufficient.

I put the box on the bed near the headboard. I heard a weird sound when I plopped it down. That prompted me to look under the pillow, covers, and mattress. There was a gun at the top of the bed under a pillow and down at the foot of the bed was a large envelope marked "To be opened in case I am dead." It was dated a couple of days before she was murdered.

I screamed, "Mike, come here!" He came flying into the room. He thought someone had been hiding in there and was attacking me.

He said, "You scared me near to death."

I apologized sheepishly for scaring him. Then I excitedly said, "Look what I found."

His eyes got really big. We sat down on the floor to carefully go through the envelope. First was a letter to her parents. We skimmed it. She thanked them for being so caring and providing her with the best childhood anyone could have. I had tears in my eyes and said, "We can't read anymore. This is too personal, and we should respect that." We carefully placed it on the bed. I know the Clumps will cherish this letter for the rest of their lives.

The second item was a small notebook. This was pure gold. Victoria had been snooping around TWC for some time now and had accumulated a lot of damning information. The notebook's entries were for the drug trade that Mr. Wilde was conducting. It showed money coming in from several different businesses that were possibly drug-cartel related. She noted the business weren't related to the shoe industry in any way.

There were entries showing money going out to, lo and behold, Andy Matthews, Sue Hastings, David Morella, and other names I didn't know. One name wasn't there that I thought might be and that was Duncan Olson's. I was so glad I almost did my happy dance. I decided to do that in my head. It also didn't include the names of all the other women who had been convinced to provide sexual services for Mr. Wilde.

Behind Andy's name was a huge question mark. This led me to believe she just came across this information. Hence her dating the envelope. I'm sure she couldn't believe Andy was part of this awful business. But this information proved it beyond any reasonable doubt.

I was wondering if some of the other names were Moe's associates. "We need to turn this over to the DEA after we've made copies of it," Mike said. "It will be their problem then."

I agreed, "We only need to show the connection between the three dumb-shit scumbag lowlifes. Pardon my potty mouth, but that is what they are."

Mike just smiled and said, "That's what they are indeed."

We looked at the last of the contents, which were copies of letters, emails, and pictures that indicated Rita hired Moe to off her two husbands so she could get their insurance money. Mr. Wilde had Moe and Rita under his thumb because he somehow had gotten a hold of these documents. He was blackmailing both of them. That is probably why Moe got him involved in the drug business to shut Mr. Wilde up. It was only a guess, but I was sure it was a good one.

I was finally putting two and two together, and now it was making sense. Victoria probably confided to Rita that she had this information. Rita went to Mr. Wilde and Moe and told them Victoria had information to blow the whistle on them. They were planning to kill Victoria, but Rita didn't want any part of that so she was beaten up and left to die in the snow. But how was Andy involved? For gosh sakes, Victoria was his fiancée. My thoughts might add up to exactly what happened.

I said, "We need to dig into Andy's and Moe's past to see what connection there is between them." Mike agreed. "But where do we start?" I asked. We looked at each other and said at the same time, "It will have to wait until we finish going through Victoria's apartment."

We continued to look for further evidence in the apartment. "I need to finish searching the bedroom and then I'll tackle the bathroom," I said. The files will have to be gone through at the station. I'm sure it contains some juicy info, but since the box is full, we will need several people's help to go through them. I didn't find anything else of importance in the bedroom.

So on to the bathroom. I went right to the medicine cabinet. I found the usual items such as aspirin, birth control pills, and an assortment of vitamins. Under the sink, I found cleaning implements for the bathroom and a small bag hidden at the back behind some bleach.

I opened it and found some of the same drugs that we found at TWC. A small note said, "I took these while Moe and Mr. Wilde were in the small office making a deal with some drug cartel jerk. I want to make sure the police believe me when I go to them. I was wearing gloves so my prints won't be on them. I'm scared, so I'm hiding this in case Mr. Wilde decides to come here and force his way in and search my place. I hope someone finds this if I'm not able to finish my plan." Poor thing, she was trying her best to get them arrested before they found out what she had been up to. No wonder she stayed late. She was gathering evidence to put them away. I'm sure it all went south for her when she saw Andy's name.

I think the last info she found before she was murdered was the documents implementing Rita. I'm now sure she wouldn't have confided in her if she had those in her possession before talking to Rita. How was she able to get it to her apartment without them seeing her? I wonder if she had help? Someone at TWC had to be involved. Someone who disliked Mr. Wilde.

Oh, I think I know who it was. Little Miss Receptionist must have seen Victoria with the info and asked her what she was doing. Being such a busybody, she wouldn't hesitate to find out what she had. Victoria probably saw an opportunity to have the help she needed.

I'm thinking we need to get a hold of Little Miss Receptionist. The last time we were at TWC, there was another woman at the reception desk. I wish I had gotten the first receptionist's name. It would make it much easier to find her. Can't ask Ms. Hastings as she hasn't been located yet. That's another mystery. Someone at TWC must have this info—Wait, we have a copy of the directory.

Now if it has "receptionist" behind her name.

Now I really am pissed at Ms. Rita. I can't wait to talk with her and see her reaction when we place her under arrest. She will need a really good lawyer to get out of murder, being an accomplice to murder on top of being part of the drug trade. God knows what other laws she had broken in her despicable life.

I had to quit thinking and take this evidence out to Mike. I didn't want him to have a near heart attack again by me screaming to get in here. He was in the midst of tearing everything out of the cupboards in the kitchen. He said there wasn't anything of importance in the rest of the room. I told him what I found in the bathroom.

We now have really important evidence along with the other items from the bedroom. He looked at it and said, "We need to get all of this to the station." I didn't argue. We quickly put everything back as it had been. We didn't want the Clumps coming into her place and finding an apartment that looked like a bomb had gone off in it. Coming here would be hard enough on them. They had to pack up all of Victoria's belongings, which would cause them more pain. We called them to let them know we had looked through her apartment, and they could come in whenever they wanted. No use using the word *searched* as it wasn't necessary.

Carting all the evidence down three flights of stairs was tiring but well worth it. Back at the station, we called Jim to come see the treasure trove of evidence we brought back. Not only Jim but everyone in the squad room gathered around while we went through the pile.

This was certainly a plentiful bounty, and it was laying on my desk. The officers who were trying to nail down evidence regarding Rita's husband's murders were elated. With this evidence, it made their case a slam dunk. They hurried off to get the arrest warrant issued. As they were running through the squad room, they shouted back, "Great work, you two."

CHAPTER EIGHT

....

Still Not Sure About Andy

WE NAILED DOWN MR. Wilde, Moe, and Sue Hastings with charges of drug trade, blackmail, and promoting prostitution. Maybe Ms. Hastings didn't participate in all the activities, but her running off certainly pointed to her being a part of this. You don't run unless you have something to hide or your guilty.

I still have several big questions circling around in my noggin. First of all, why did Andy get involved? He didn't work for TWC. How did he become a serious part of the illegal operation? Why did he ask Victoria to marry him? Why get involved with someone you had to either leave behind or kill? But the biggest conundrum is the relationship between him and Moe. I'm sure finding that connection will lead us to the answers of all these questions.

I told Mike, "We need to start at the beginning." Finding out where they both were born will probably help a lot. They aren't close to the same age. Moe is probably about fifteen years older than Andy. So, they couldn't have met in school. I'm really sure Moe didn't attend a college or university. They don't have the same last name. Knowing where they were born might provide the answer we are looking for.

Mike said he would check Washington's vital statistics for a birth record for Andy. I didn't know where to look for Morella, but it sounded like an Italian name so I would start checking for birth records in New York state. This was going to be a long and boring search. I punched in "David Morella" and the internet started searching. I went to get a cup of coffee and asked if Mike wanted me to bring him one. He nodded his head in the affirmative. It only took a couple of minutes, and when I got back to my desk, the computer was still grinding away.

Mike said Andy was born in Vancouver, Washington. He had the address and would see if the parents were still there. He searched the online white pages for the Matthews listed on the birth certificate. This would tell if they were still living in Vancouver at that address. As luck would have it, they weren't there. He looked at all the other Matthews listed, but no one had the same first names.

He wondered if the University of Washington had an emergency contact list. If they did, maybe it would have the names of who to contact in case of an emergency. He called the registrar's office. They said they would check but would have to get back to him as their computers, as they put it, were throwing a fit at the moment. He gave them his phone number and hung up. He told me what they said and a laugh bubbled up. I couldn't help but let it out. With that, Mike started to chuckle too.

My search wasn't going any better. I checked the vital statistics in New York and there were Morellas listed but, none had David as the baby's name. Maybe Illinois or New Jersey would be my next search. Mike interrupted my thought process and said we should go get something to eat. It was late and he was starving. There is a good hole-in-the-wall located near the station. I said, "Just a minute," and plugged in my search for New Jersey and we left.

I didn't realize just how hungry I was until we entered the place. The smells were amazing. I sat down at the first booth and grabbed a menu. Mike looked at me and said, "Well, we could have gone a little farther into the diner."

He really didn't like sitting close to the door. A lot of police are paranoid about their backs to doors or not being able to see the door. I got up with the menu in hand and said no problem. We moved to a corner booth facing the entrance. The waitress knew Mike and came over smiling. "How you doing, Mike?" she said.

"Hi, Vivian," he answered. "I'm hungry, so what do you have for the special tonight?" She said meatloaf, mashed potatoes and gravy, mixed vegetables served with a great mixed green salad.

"YUM," I said out loud, "I will have that." No wonder the smells were so inviting.

Mike just grinned and said, "Bring me that too." She asked what we would like to drink and I said lemonade. Mike ordered coffee. I probably should have gotten that too as it would be a long night.

Vivian asked me for the menu I still was clutching in my hand. I'm way too hungry and tired. I gave it to her, and she took it back to its rightful place. We were quiet except for an occasional "do you think" or "what about that." The food came and you could have heard a pin drop. There was no conversation. We just ate and savored every bite. I couldn't believe I ate everything on the plate. My stomach was so full I couldn't even drink another sip of my lemonade. Vivian came over to refill Mike's coffee and asked if we wanted desert. I wanted it, but I asked myself where would I put it.

I said without thinking, "What do you have?"

Mike looked at me with his mouth open then said, "Do you have hollow legs or something?"

I replied, "I'm going to take it back to the station with me. I can't pass up desert especially since the food here is exceptionally good." Vivian smiled and named off what was left. I selected the coconut cream pie as it was my favorite. I asked if she would top off my lemonade and put in a paper cup so I can take it with me.

She said no problem and then asked with a critical look in her eye, "When was the last time you ate?" I really couldn't remember, so I said, "I think this morning." She looked at me, shook her head, and went to get the pie and a container for my drink. When she got back, the piece of pie was huge. She said, "Now you eat all of it. You need it," and closed the box.

We got our bills and Mike grabbed mine. He said it was his treat. I could get the next one. I thanked him and said, "Can we come back tomorrow?" Both he and Vivian laughed. I said, "No, I'm serious. I can't remember eating food this good since I left home. My mother cooks food like you serve here, and boy do I miss it." Mike shrugged his shoulders and said he'd think about coming back.

Vivian said, "Honey, you can come back any time you want. I love to see a woman who isn't afraid to eat a good meal without worrying about the calories."

I said, "I worry but there isn't a calorie I can't burn off." She laughed and walked back to the register. I grabbed my pie and lemonade and happily walked back to the station with Mike. He was smiling all the way back.

Since I was refueled, I was ready to tackle the job again. I turned on my computer as it had gone to sleep. I was surprised to find Moe's birth records looking back at me. "I found Moe," I said. Mike came over, and we saw he was born in Hoboken, New Jersey. The address was listed along with the parents' names. It would be way too late now to call the number listed. So, first thing tomorrow I would see if they still lived there.

He went back to check the message on his phone. Mike listened to his message. He got up and said the U of W didn't have that information. Another dead end. Well, maybe tomorrow when we talk with momma and papa Morella we will get some answers. Right now, my pie is calling my name. When I opened the box, it was still filling the whole area. I asked, "Are you interested in sharing some of this pie with me?"

Mike got up, headed to our little kitchen, and brought back two paper plates and forks. He said, "I thought you'd never ask. Coconut cream it my favorite too." We ate and hashed over some of the evidence trying to glean more out of the contents. I couldn't help it, I yawned and said, "I need to call it a night before I just lay my head on the desk and pass out." We both were dead tried. We retrieved our coats and walked out together.

I was concerned for Mike. He had just lost his dad, and I wasn't sure how he was going to be when he got home. I asked if he would to be alright tonight. He said he would, but it was nice of me to be concerned. We got in our cars and headed to our respective domiciles. As I drove away, I was thinking there is always tomorrow and having three scumbags in jail was a great finish to a long day.

CHAPTER NINE

....

Interrogations, I Love Them!

DRIVING HOME, I WAS thinking that tomorrow we would be able to start interrogating all of them. Mr. Wilde should be awake and not high on meds. We might even be able to have him transported to the station for grilling. I was looking forward to that.

Moe and Andy are in their cells stewing, and they should be about ready to boil over. Sometimes it pays to let them simmer before stirring the pot. I want to be there with all three of them when the questions start flying. I know I have some duzzies to ask.

Finally, I'm home, showered, well feed, and flopping onto bed. No questions or theories running around my brain tonight. Just cuddling into the sheets and blankets. Lights out and loving this! I guess a full stomach and apprehending the creeps, not to mention having a lot of questions answered, is the way for a good night's sleep.

The next morning, I'm awake and up early and very well rested. A trip to the kitchen to eat before I get ready for the day.

Darn, it looks like I'm headed to Starbucks again. The coffee is all gone and the bread that is left is starting to grow penicillin. How can mold become a medicine that cures all sorts of diseases? Gross is what I call it. This isn't something to dwell on as I don't have time to waste. I shower, get dressed, put a little bit of makeup on, and I'm ready to go.

Back at work and I am so looking forward to making the three scumbags sweat more. I have a million questions. At that moment,

I remember I need to call the Morellas. I hope they are home and willing to talk to me. Especially after telling them who I am and why I'm calling.

The phone is ringing. I'm about to hang up when someone picks up. The person says hello, and I'm sure it is Mrs. Morella. I say hello and introduce myself. There was a second before she said, "What did Moe do now?"

I said that I was sorry to say he was in jail on suspicion of murder and a lot of other charges. I could hear her moan a little. I said, "I am really sorry to bother you, but we need to get some information." She agreed right away that she would be willing to tell us anything we needed if she could. She said she was expecting a call like this one, one of these days. I asked if he had been in trouble before. She said almost all of his life. They tried to get him help several times, but it was useless.

"What did he do?" I asked.

She said it would be easier to say what he didn't do. After hesitating a little, she said he had swiped little things to begin with. Then he got into selling drugs and stealing to supply his habit. He stole cars and started a prostitution ring. He was eventually caught and went to prison. When he got out, she said, "We told him he wasn't welcome any more in their home or for that matter in the state."

I then asked if she ever heard of Andy Matthews. She said she has a cousin who lives in Vancouver in Washington state. She had a son with that name. She wasn't sure where her cousin moved to but was sure she was still in Washington somewhere. She continued, "After Moe left, he went out there so people wouldn't know what he was. I warned Trudy, my cousin, about him. I guess she didn't believe me. Is Andy involved too?"

I said, "I'm afraid so."

She sighed and said, "I'm so sorry. I guess having a child later in life wasn't such a good idea after all. My husband died a couple of years ago, and before he died, he said he was hoping that Moe had change for my sake. I told him not to worry because I have a lot of great friends and he had done well by me. You don't have to sugarcoat anything," she said, "when you are talking to Moe. He knows what I think of him."

I said, "Thank you for your honest replies, and I'm so sorry you didn't have the son you both wanted."

She said, "Thank you, dear," and hung up.

Mike came into the station while I was talking or, should say, listening to Mrs. Morella. When I hung up, I said, "I have the connection between those two in the cells upstairs. Andy is Moe's cousin." I told him about the trouble Moe had been in and the prison time. Mrs. Morella said they tried several times to get help for him, but he was a bad egg—my version, not her exact words.

Mike said he was glad I called. "I'm sure it was easier talking with you rather than to a man."

"Well, she wasn't sorry I called. She was expecting a call like this one, one of these days. Her exact words. Now we have the connection, we need to find out why Andy went along with Moe," I said.

I asked, "Is Mr. Wilde here, or do we need to go to the hospital to question him?"

Mike answered, "They are transporting him over to us right now."

I asked, "Are you ready to start interrogating them?" He looked at me and said he was really ready. He wanted them wrapped up so tight they couldn't even wiggle their big toe.

We headed to the interrogation rooms. First up was Andy. Mike figured he would be the easiest one to crack. I wasn't so sure. Jim wanted to be included, but another case came in that he needed his attention. He said, "Go get them wrapped up," in no uncertain terms. I'm not going to sugarcoat what he said. His actual words were "Get those bastards."

"That is our plan," we told him.

We came in and Andy stood up. He was mad as a wet hen. He started yelling at us that we had no right to hold him overnight and treat him the way we did. Mike calmly said, "Sit down before I help you sit." Of course, he didn't want Mike putting him in his chair, so he sat down. Mike said, "Let me draw you a verbal map so you know just why you are here. First, you were in the company of Moe and

Mr. Wilde in Moe's cabin. You all shot at police officers while resisting arrest. Second, your Jeep was there as you and Moe drove up to the cabin together. The lot attendant where your trailer is stored gave us that info. We have your trailer and Moe's Corvette in our garage. Our techs have gone over them with a fine-tooth comb. In Moe's trunk, we found Victoria's blood, boot, and fingernails. We also found Victoria's blood in Moe's condo. You were a frequent visitor there along with Mr. Wilde. The condo manager is an eyewitness and gave your description and Mr. Wilde's to our sketch artist. We have them, and they are really good likenesses. Third, we have an eyewitness to your comings and goings at the Wilde Company, and you weren't there to just see Victoria. Fourth, we found out that you and Moe are cousins. These facts add up to your arrest and being held in jail. Now do you think you are ready to answer our questions?"

Andy had his head in his hands and mumbled yes.

"Why did you get involved with Victoria? Didn't you know that it would put her in harm's way?" I asked.

He said he didn't think that was possible. He really loved Victoria, and when Moe murdered her, he lost it. Moe had to give him some kind of drug to get him to settled down.

Mike asked, "How did Moe get you involved in his slimy ways?"

Andy answered he needed the money to continue going to school. It was getting harder and harder to come up with the tuition. He already had enormous student loans to pay off. Moe said he wouldn't have to do anything except to distribute drugs to students at the U of W.

Moe also told him to get Duncan Olson involved in taking pictures at TWC. He needed pictures of people attending the shoots and parties. He wanted to blackmail them so he needed the pictures of them doing bad things to use. I asked, "Like the ladies doing sexual favors for some of the attendees?"

He said, "Yes, I think that was one of the things he wanted. Moe wanted to get other things too." I asked what were they. He thought maybe some of the attendees were using some of the drugs, and he wanted to blackmail them for that. Okay, that would do it.

Moe also told him to call an associate of Mr. Wilde and have him call Duncan Olson to see if he would like to do a photo shoot at the Wilde Company. Duncan was thrilled to have the chance to have his name on the advertisements. Andy knew Duncan was an excellent photographer and told Mr. Wilde he should hire him. After they both recommended Duncan, Mr. Wilde called him and Duncan accepted the opportunity.

I asked, "Did Duncan know the part about shooting lurid pictures?" Andy said no.

We asked, "Was this person you called also one of Moe's associates?"

"Yes."

"What is this person's name?"

"His name is Craig Douglas."

We heard of him but never could pin anything on him. I was wondering how Duncan knew this person. That question would have to wait until we saw Mr. Olson again. I told Andy to go on. He said Mr. Wilde was involved already in the drug trade. His business was a good front for shipping and receiving drugs. Moe wanted in on that too. So, he needed to get some info he could use to nail Mr. Wilde down. Andy heard from Victoria about Mr. Wilde being a womanizer and making the ladies supply sexual favors. He told Moe, and with that information, he approached Rita to get the ladies to start charging for their services. Rita did it because Moe had done some bad things for her that would get her into a lot of trouble.

We asked if he knew that Victoria was one of these ladies. He said he didn't at first, but one night she was crying and he asked why. She told him what was going on and that now Moe was requiring her to sleep with some of his associates. She told him she had already told Mr. Wilde he wouldn't be getting anymore sexual favors from her. She would tell Mrs. Wilde if he forced her to do it anymore. She also had some other information she would use.

I said, "You knew she had this info?"

He said, "Yes, but not exactly what it was." I was thinking it was about his drug deals, but he didn't think it included him. She finally told him it was regarding Mr. Wilde's drug business, but she didn't indicate anyone else. Andy said he wanted to get out too and told Moe.

Mike asked, "What exactly did you tell Moe?"

"I told him because Victoria and I were engaged she didn't want to do the sexual favors anymore, and I didn't want her doing it either. I told him I wouldn't be selling drugs anymore either."

"You didn't actually know how Victoria knew about the drug deals?"

"She didn't tell me how she knew about Mr. Wilde's drug dealings, and I didn't ask her. I guess I should have. I could have possibly helped her."

"Now to ask the hardest question. Did you know Moe was planning to kill Victoria?"

"Hell, no!" he shouted. "I wasn't with either of them that night. I was studying at the library and then at the apartment. I got in really late, so Duncan didn't know I was there. I didn't want to wake him so I was very quiet. I never lied about that. The first I heard about Victoria being murdered is when you told me. All the time you were talking, I was thinking it was that bastard Moe. I was sure it was him. He didn't like anyone telling him they were done with what he called his business dealings. Now it made sense to me why his demeanor was so cold."

Mike finally said, "So why were you with Moe the next day?"

Andy said he called him right after he got back to his room. He told us he called Moe every name in the book then hung up. "I was boiling mad and didn't know what to do. My cell rang and I saw Moe's name on the caller ID. I answered it because I didn't want to have Duncan coming in to see if I was alright. Moe told me to get my ass over to the condo or he would call the police and anonymously tell them about my drug dealing. I told him it would look bad to Duncan if I left right after hearing about Victoria. He said damn he knows about that already. He mumbled something and said come early in the morning. He said to park the SUV far from the condo. I was wondering what he meant by Duncan knows about that already."

Well, we did go over there right after we left the Clumps. But how did Moe know about that?

I said, "What happened when you went there?"

Andy said, "Moe roughed me up where it didn't show. When he got tired of smacking me around, I was still angry and asked him why he murdered Victoria. He said he found out she had been spying on them and was planning on going to the police. I asked how he found out. He said he put a little pressure on the person helping her plus there were pencil light cameras installed in the cabinets. I asked if it was Rita. He told me it was Sarah, the quiet receptionist. He said she won't be talking anytime soon or maybe never. Then he told me we are driving to the storage lot and getting my Jeep."

I was puzzled as it was in Andy's name. I asked about that.

He said, "Moe didn't want the Jeep in his name because he could use it as a getaway vehicle. No one would associate it with him."

Okay, that makes sense. "Then what did he do?"

"Moe said he had called Mr. Wilde late last night and told him to meet us at the cabin in the morning. I asked him about Rita, 'Don't you want her there too?' He said, 'Don't worry about her. I took care of her too.'"

Mike asked if he was in any other part of the condo.

"No, I was just in the living room. He wouldn't even let me use the bathroom. I was getting scared because I finally knew what he was capable of."

Mike said, "What happened at the storage lot?"

Andy said, "He parked his car on the other side of my trailer. He went into the trailer and brought out a bag. I didn't know what was in it." I asked what the bag looked like. Andy said it was just a black overnight bag.

"Moe had some cloths in the trailer, so I thought he was bringing some of them with us."

"Continue," I said.

"We got in the Jeep and headed to the cabin. I said, 'Do we need any food?' and Moe said don't worry about that. The rest of the way we both were quiet. I was getting more nervous all the time."

I asked, "What happened when you got to the cabin?"

He said, "Mr. Wilde was already there. He was pacing back and forth as he didn't have a key to get in. Mr. Wilde yelled at Moe for taking his sweet time getting up there. Moe just laughed and told him to hold his jockstrap. Mr. Wilde yelled, 'We need to go back to the company and get everything out of there.' Moe told him there was plenty of time to do that. He had other plans right now. So, we all went into the cabin. Moe went over to the kitchen sink and dumped the clothes that were in the bag into some hot water. I saw red blotches and knew that was some of Victoria's blood. I started to cry. Moe screamed at me to shut up and get some coffee going. He looked at Mr. Wilde and motioned him to go outside. They went out of the cabin. They came back in about ten minutes later. Mr. Wilde was sort of a gray color and holding his side. I'm sure Moe did to him what he did to me. We sat and drank coffee while Moe was thinking things over.

"Then we heard the bullhorn telling us to come out with our hands up. Moe yelled at us to get the guns and start shooting. I ran behind the couch as I didn't want any part of that. Moe took a shot at me, but it didn't penetrate the couch. Luckily for me, there were shots coming from outside. Moe ran from the front to the other side of the room shooting all the while. Mr. Wilde ran to the back of the cabin and took a couple of shots. Then I heard him scream, 'I've been shot.' Moe decided we were outgunned and threw his gun out the window. I hadn't fired mine, but I wasn't going out that door with it in my hands. So I threw mine out too. Then we all walked out the door. You know the rest."

Mike and I sat back and looked at Andy. We were sure he was telling the truth. To make sure, I asked him to raise his shirt. There were black and blue marks all over his torso. I told him that was what we needed to see. We had the police officer escort him back to his cell. I said, "Make sure he isn't in with David Morella." He nodded his head and took away his charge.

I said, "We need to have all three guns checked, but I'm sure the one with Andy's prints wasn't fired recently.'

Mike agreed. He said, "I wonder if Captain Bob noticed the bullet hole on the couch. We could call him to dig it out to see if it matches the bullets fired from Moe's gun."

"I'm with you on that one," I said. We called Jim to ask Captain Bob if he could have an officer go out to retrieve the slug.

He said, "No problem, but why do you need it?"

We did a little explaining without going into a lot of detail. He understood and would call right away if they found it.

We waited about thirty minutes for Captain Bob's answer. Sure enough, the couch had a bullet lodged in it. So probably one of the guns wasn't fired either. They all needed to be all gone over for gunpowder residue.

CHAPTER TEN

·····················

Now to Put Moe Over
the Hot Coals

WE HAD MORE AMMUNITION to question Moe with. He was brought into the interrogation room. Of course, he was accompanied by an attorney. We smiled and said, "We only have a few questions." I told him, "By the way, your mother told me some interesting things."

He got really mad and started to get up. Both his attorney and Mike stood up and told him to sit down. He said, "That bitch can rot in hell." His attorney said, "Shut up."

I chimed in with "Don't talk about your mother that way." I wanted to add *weasel*, but I held my tongue.

Mike asked him if he knew Mr. Wilde. He looked at the attorney, and he nodded in the affirmative. Moe said he knew him. Then Mike added Andy's name. He shouted, "That ungrateful cousin could also rot in hell."

"Well, that is an affirmative," I said. At this point, Moe's attorney was glaring at him. I said, "We don't need to ask if you knew Victoria or Rita because we have evidence of their blood on your clothes."

The attorney said, "That evidence wouldn't be allowed in court as you forced your way into the cabin."

I informed him that we had warrants for their arrests. We also had ones that allowed us to search all their properties. At hearing that, Moe started to wilt. Just to clear things up for the attorney, after the three men—and I used that term lightly—were done shooting at us they came out of the cabin with their hands up. We didn't force our way into the cabin.

We then asked Moe, "Does the name Craig Douglas ring a bell?"

He looked surprised, but his attorney jumped in and said, "You don't have to answer that questions."

I looked right at him and asked, "Why? Is there something Mr. Douglas does that Moe doesn't want to be associated with?" He just got up, grabbed Moe's arm, and said, "We are done here."

Mike also stood up and said, "Yes, Moe is well done. So it doesn't matter if you take him out of here. Although, we might be able to take the death penalty off the table if Moe gives us the information we need." With that statement, Moe's mouth fell open.

"Death penalty," he said.

Mike said yes. "You killed one women and possibly another. We haven't found Sarah yet. And there is Rita who is undergoing her third operation."

At that, Moe turned a little green and said weakly, "She is alive."

"Yes," I said. "She is holding on, and when she is fully able to speak with us, she will fry you."

The attorney said, "That's enough."

Moe yelled, "She had me kill her two husbands. Are you going to believe her?"

His attorney hung his head and said, "I'm done. You can find another attorney to defend you. You open your mouth and put your foot in it without the detectives asking you one question." He got up and left.

Mike said, "Amy, I believe Moe is in need of another attorney."

He just sat there. He finally said, "What do you want to know?"

"First off, did Rita have anything to do with Victoria's murder?"

He replied no. "She came back to help her, and I forced my way in behind her. She started to scream, but I knocked her out. I got Victoria and I threw her in my trunk. Before that, I tied Rita up and took her keys."

I said, "We know what you did to Victoria. Why did you go back for Rita?"

"Because I knew she would rat on me to save herself. I brought Victoria back and put her next to her car so it would look like she got mugged. I then went in and got Rita. She put up a struggle, so I knocked her out again and put her in her trunk and drove to Carkeek Park. I worked her over some more and left her. I thought she would die before anyone found her. I had a change of clothes with me, so I threw the bloody clothes in the bag and changed quickly. I was so worked up I didn't even feel the cold. I walked back up to Third and hitched a ride."

The detectives who were compiling info on Rita's late husband's came in and said, "While you are in the mood to confess, please tell us how you managed to murder Rita's husbands."

Moe asked, "Are these confessions tied into the deal we make on not getting the death penalty?" We looked at the detectives and they said, "Hell, why not? We need the details."

Moe said he was in need of cash and went to Mr. Douglas. Craig was living in Magnolia right across the street from Rita. She told him she was having difficulty with husband number one. Craig had a thing for Rita and said he would get help for her. "Two days later, I met up with her and told her I would do it for twenty thousand. She said that was a bargain, but it needed to look like an accident. I said no problem. I asked her what car he drove, and she said the Cadillac. I told her to leave the garage door unlocked and ajar so I could fix the car to look like it crashed because of faulty parts.

"Rita agreed and told me to come by on Thursday night. She played cards with a group of ladies, and she would be coming home late. She knew her husband would be sleeping. So that took care of number one. With the insurance money, she moved closer to the bluff and soon met another bachelor. They were married for only six months before she got bored with him. She approached me again and said there would be another twenty thousand if I wanted the job. I told her it would look suspicious if this one happened so soon after the first husband's death. She said, 'Don't wait too long.'

"I asked what Mr. Rawlins liked to do so I could plan this accident. She said, 'He flies a lot. He has a plane at the Renton Boeing airfield. I will give you where the airplanes is located, the model of the plane, and what his schedule is for the next six months. But don't wait too long.' I asked her for a picture of him and his plane so I wouldn't make a slipup. She met me at the same restaurant and supplied all the data I needed for the job."

Both detectives said, "We have all the information we need to take to the prosecuting attorney. He will love what we have learned. Thank you for the information." Moe just grunted.

They left and I spoke up. I asked, "How did you become Rita's boyfriend?"

He said he told her she would have to do everything he said after the second murder. He told her he had a recording of each time she requested his services. There were papers with everything spelled out and pictures. "I told her we need to look like we were dating so no one would become suspicious. Then I asked her to get something I could use against Mr. Wilde. I knew he was dealing drugs because Craig was in on it and let that slip. Craig was dangerous, and I didn't want to double-cross him, so I figured Mr. Wilde was the perfect patsy.

"Rita told me about his blackmailing them into going to bed with him. I figured that was the perfect way to get to him. I told Rita to tell all the ladies I had a plan for them to get back at him. She kept her end of the bargain and told them I could help. Of course, they were all suckers, and I got some extra dough out of it. That was on top of blackmailing Mr. Wilde and making me a partner in his side business."

I asked, "Why get Andy involved?"

"You know he is family," he said, "and he needed some extra cash for school. It was easy to bring him in. The one thing I didn't expect was him falling for Victoria and getting engaged. I had to put a stop to that. I told Mr. Wilde to install some pencil light cameras in the three cabinets. Then I told him to leave all of the doors open while he went to do something else. That is how we found out she was snooping. She took some files out of boxes and some pictures and put them in another file box. We didn't know she had help until we saw her talking with Sarah. I saw her asking Sarah if she would help put the files in her car."

I asked why Mr. Wilde hadn't seen the files in her apartment. Moe answered that Veronica had already gotten information on Mr. Wilde and told him she would use it if he kept making her sleep with him. She said her apartment was off limits to him, and she had a new lock system installed on her entry door. That way we couldn't bother her anymore. Then she called me and said she wouldn't take care of my associates and wanted her money back. That's when I knew I had to work fast before she spilled all the beans to Andy.

Mike asked, "Why did you beat up Andy? Were you planning on killing him? Andy told us he was sure that murdering him was your plan."

Moe just shrugged and said, "Taking care of business. I was going to off both of them, but I wanted to make them squirm before doing it. Then all hell broke loose. You damn cops." With that comment, we knew we had as much out of him as we were going to get.

I had this nagging feeling there was something else I wanted to find out. Then it dawned on me. I asked, "Why didn't you finish Rita off instead of leaving her there half alive?"

He said letting her freeze to death was poetic justice. I must have looked puzzled, so he said, "I was paying her back for always being ice cold toward me." He looked at both of us and said, "I'm not saying another word," folded his arms across his chest, and glared at us.

Mike looked at me and we both laughed. It was the most satisfying thing I felt in a long time. When we were ready to leave, we were still laughing. We got up, waved to the guard to come take the scumbag back to his cell, and left.

CHAPTER ELEVEN

....

Sarah, Nicole, and Mr. Wilde—Mystery Solved

WHILE WE WERE INTERROGATING Moe, a call came in from Harborview. When we got back to our desks, I saw my message light blinking. I put the phone on speaker so Mike could hear the message. Dr. Richter said, "You won't believe this, but another lady was brought into the emergency ward. She said a man named Moe had beaten her badly. After doing the triage, I found she had a concussion, broken ribs, and several large contusions. Maybe more internal damage I can't see. The person dropping her off didn't leave her name, but she looked a lot like Mrs. Wilde. I thought you would like to know."

I got on the phone and asked to speak to Dr. Richter. I told the nurse I was returning her call. She told me she would get her right away. Dr. Richter came on the line very quickly. I asked how Sarah was doing and could we speak with her. Dr. Richter said, "She is in ICU but awake. She had a collapsed lung as well as the other injuries I was able to see. I'm positive she wants to talk with you. As a matter of fact, she has been asking for you personally for the last hour."

I asked just out of curiosity, "How did you know it was Mrs. Wilde?"

She said, "When Mr. Wilde was brought in, she came running into the emergency ward wanting to know where he was. I had to calm her down and she sat for an hour or so in here. Naturally, I got a good look at her. I told Dr. Richter we will be up there as soon as we wrap some things up at the station." I thanked her and hung up.

Mike was listening and looking at me the whole time I was talking to the doc. He said, "Well I'll be damned." After I hung up, we talked about the whole conversation and his only question was why and how did Mrs. Wilde know Sarah was injured. I said, "You've got me. I can't make a connection either." Mike immediately got on the phone and call her.

She answered soon after the first ring. Mike was blunt and asked how she knew Sarah was injured. She said, "Sarah Lou was her sister, and they talked every day. Yesterday, she didn't call. I was really worried especially since I found out all the bad things my soon-to-be ex-husband was doing." The weather had cleared up so she was able to drive to Sarah Lou's apartment. "I found her on the couch holding her stomach, and there was an ice bag on her head. I didn't wait for Sarah Lou to tell me what happened. I gently got her in the car and drove like crazy to Harborview."

Mike thanked her for the information and said he was glad she knew Sarah and was able to help her. Then he hung up and told me Sarah and Mrs. Wilde were sisters. I was shocked. "I would never have guessed," I said. Sarah was okay looking while her sister was absolutely stunning. "Wow, that really blows me away. I had no idea they were related." Mike said he wouldn't have made the connection either. "I'll never know why Mr. Wilde had to have affairs on the side when his wife is so gorgeous." Mike nodded and added, "Some men are never satisfied. Not all but some."

We headed to Harborview to see Sarah. I asked Mike if we could look in on Rita while we are there. I want to see how she likes being cuffed to a hospital bed. Mike said, "Boy, I really don't ever want to piss you off."

I laughed and said, "You haven't murdered anyone so that will never happen."

He snickered and said, "I am so relieved."

Once at the hospital, we checked in on Rita. It would be a quick in and out because I didn't want to do more physical harm to her.

Instead, I was smiling at her all the time, and Rita just lay there glaring at us. I simply said, "You should have call the police to tell them what was going on. Maybe then you wouldn't be in the hospital." The glare continued. "Oh well, you deserve all you're going to get," I said as we walked out.

Mike said, "I'm glad you contained yourself."

I said, "The smiling helped a lot."

We headed directly to the ICU. Since we were police officers, we were admitted without question. Normally only close relatives are permitted to visit there. We were shown to Sarah's bed. I asked her how she was doing. Without hesitation, she asked if we had Mr. Wilde and Moe in custody. I said, "Yes, we do, and they aren't going anywhere for a long time." She sighed said she was alright now.

We asked her how she got involved in all this craziness. She said, "Victoria came by my desk one evening a few minutes after closing. She had a bunch of files and other items in boxes. She said she needed help getting them to her car. I asked, 'What in the world do you have?' She said evidence she wanted to get to the police regarding bad things that were going on here at the company. I naturally heartily agreed to help. Moe was in the building at the time, and he must have seen us taking the boxes out. If I'd known he was watching, I would have never agreed to help. At first, he wasn't so bad, but the longer he was hanging around the company, the more he gave me the creeps. He was always snooping around and always said the most off-colored things about the women and Mr. Wilde. I didn't like that even though Brad is a pig."

"Brad?" I said puzzled.

"Oh, Brad is Mr. Wilde's first name."

I saw Sarah was getting agitated, so I changed the subject. I asked how she came to work for Mr. Wilde. She said, "I came to Seattle from our hometown. I didn't have a job lined up, and it was during a time when jobs were scarce. Nicole asked her dumb shit husband Brad to help me out. I never trusted him. I don't know what my sister saw in him and to go ahead and marry the scumbag. I tried to warn her, but she didn't listen. I guess she saw something. If

I had known what a scumbag he really was, I would have starved first before going to work there."

Mike nudged me and said, "I think we have all the information we need for now. You rest and we will call Nicole and let her know she can visit you. She was really worried about you." I said, "Take care and thank you for helping us with this case."

She beamed and said, "No, thank you, guys. I can rest easy now."

We needed to talk with Nicole anyway so we called and asked if we could come by. She agreed and said, "I'm not going anywhere today. I don't even want to show my face outside my home." I told her to hang in there, things will get better.

We got to her house about 2:00 p.m. We didn't want to upset her, but we needed a little more information. She answered the door and was a bit of a mess. I felt really sorry for her. I decided to let her know that Sarah was out of danger and looking much better. She could visit her any time, I said and added they will probably be moving her to another room soon. That lifted her spirits a little.

Her first comment was, "Why is this all happening?"

We told her, "Let's go into the living room and sit down." She nodded and lead the way.

Mike asked her if she had any inkling that the Wilde Company was a front for illegal drug trade. She started to cry and said, "No, how could I be so stupid?" I assured her that this wasn't her fault. She said she was afraid that she and the boys would be out in the cold. Mike wanted to assure her and said that won't happen. It looks like all the money gotten from the drug trade was stored at the warehouse.

"All the money in your bank accounts was from legal dealings of the Wilde Company. The books were kept separate. I'm sure your husband loved you and the boys and didn't want this side of him to harm you. Your accountant had no idea there was another set of books. They were kept in a small office in the warehouse. It seems the only other person who knew about the other business was Ms. Hastings. We're not sure how she fits in, but we will find out. This is one of the reasons we are here. Did you know her very well?"

Nicole answered that she was at several parties and the designer shows. She seemed nice but didn't mingle much with other employees. The only person she ever saw her mingle with much was Rita.

Why does Rita keep popping up in the scenario? I wondered. "I'm sure there must have been someone else," I said.

Nicole thought for a moment and said, "There was another man. I believe his name was Douglas or something like that."

Now we had another connection to Mr. Douglas. The Feds have been trying to pin something on him for some time now. He has been on our radar too. Maybe we can finally have enough on him with these connections.

I knew Nicole was hopelessly lost. To get her feeling more secure, I told her she was listed on the company's incorporation documents as a co-owner.

She looked at me stunned. "Are you sure?" she asked.

"Yes, definitely sure. I believe if you have a good head for business, you will be able to run the Wilde Company. You probably will improve it. Put the woman's touch on it, you know. If you feel uncomfortable, just hire a few people who have already worked in the industry. They will help get you moving forward. I'm sure there are people you've met at designer shows. They might have approached Mr. Wilde to hire them. If you have an attendee list from those shows people's names might pop out at you or Mr. Wilde might have mentioned them in passing to you. Your boys also need to be involved. Let them help grow the business. Start them in the warehouse or factory. Working their way up will give them a better appreciation for the business. Remember, someday it will be theirs. I'm also sure the salesladies would be glad to have a job to come back to. What happened wasn't their fault. Sarah can probably be a big help too. She seems quite competent and she loves you."

After this pep talk, Nicole was feeling much stronger. Her shoulders were squared, and she didn't have teary eyes. Before we left, Mike told her, "Your boys will need you more now than they ever have. Make sure you let them know what is going on so they can handle what is bound to come their way."

She said she would. "They are staying with some friends at their cabin right now. They will be skiing and having fun. That is what I wanted for them right now. Thank God for my best friends. They aren't judgmental and are there for all of us. Right now, I plan to clean up and then go see my sister."

"Good idea." I said "And if you need support from us, please call. Goodbye for now," we said.

I started talking as soon as we were in the car. "Can you believe that Nicole had no idea about the bad things going on at TWC?" Mike nodded his head in the affirmative. Most of the time spouses are the last to have a clue about the extracurricular things their other halves are up to.

We had a case where the husband was murdering prostitutes and the wife didn't know a thing. That is pretty sad when you think about it. I remembered that case, and it still sends a chill up my spine. "I hope I never have to deal with something like that."

Mike smiled and said, "Just pick the right guy and you won't have to worry."

I said, "But you really don't know the person you are dating. They always show their good side, don't they?"

He just shrugged his shoulders and said, "Pick someone you have gotten close to. Stay away from guys who seem too good to be true."

We put our conversation hold as we were both starving. I suggested the hole-in-the-wall again, and Mike swung the car in that direction. We entered the diner and Vivian was working again. The aroma was just as amazing as the first time I was here. We took a place in the same booth. I grabbed a menu and went right to the dinner section. Mike just yelled, "What's on the special tonight?"

Vivian came over and said, "Were you born in a barn? Don't yell. I was on my way over." Mike just grinned. Vivian sighed and said, "We have real roasted turkey with stuffing, potatoes and gravy, mixed vegetables, and a side of cranberry sauce."

"No salad and rolls?" Mike asked.

"You are going to bust if you add a salad, but yes one roll does come with the meal," Vivian answered.

I spoke up and said, "I would like a hamburger with bacon and mozzarella cheese on it. Does it come with fries too?"

Vivian nodded yes and asked, "What kind of fries do you want? Steak, stick fries, beer battered, or sweet potato?"

"I want the beer-battered fries and a side of tartar. Add a vanilla shake with it please."

I guess Vivian was used to my appetite as she just nodded and looked at Mike. He ordered the special with a salad and ranch dressing. We sat in silence while waiting for our dinner to arrive. It seems like we have been talking all day and didn't have anything else to say.

Dinner arrived and we dived into it like starving animals. Well, maybe not quite that bad. I was starving since once again we hadn't had time for lunch. We finished eating and I grabbed the bill. Mike started to complain, and I reminded him of our agreement that I would pay for the next round. I paid and we headed for the station.

Sitting at my desk doing nothing but letting my dinner settle, I started thinking. I know the case is coming close to being wrapped up, but there is still another hurdle to overcome, interrogating Mr. Wilde, aka the dumb shit. Tightwad just didn't fit him anymore.

I always had a bad feeling about him. Now I know my feelings were right on the nose. I was going to love making him squirm during the interrogation tomorrow. My hope was he had stewed long enough. He was probably wondering what we knew and what we are going to ask. Mike was sitting quietly. He finally said, "Tomorrow we have the last scumbag to interrogate." I agreed and told him what I had been thinking. He nodded and sat there. He finally got up and said, "I'll walk with you to the garage." We were both beat and ready to go home. Jim stopped us before we got too far.

He said, "I called the FBI and told them we were interrogating Mr. Wilde tomorrow. They want anything we get on Craig Douglas."

I was very happy to hear that. It is another plus in grilling Mr. Wilde. We might get another criminal off the streets. We nodded yes and walked out.

I woke up and remembered I hadn't gone grocery shopping again for the millionth time. Maybe that is way over the actual count but it feels like it. Well, I'll hit Starbucks again tomorrow morning. I should own stock in it. I'm probably their best customer, and if this keeps up, I'll have to get a loan. Oh well, I might as well keep them employed. I'm getting a more substantial breakfast this time thought.

I showered, dressed, applied a little makeup, and headed for the door. Wouldn't you know it, the phone rang. I couldn't ignore it because it might be in connection with the case.

I answered and a strange man's voice said, "We know where you live, so you better back off Mr. Wilde."

I said, "I don't know what you are talking about," and hung up. I quickly dialed Mike. I told him about the call I just got. He said, "Don't leave. I'm on my way to pick you up. I'll call and have a patrol car on the way too."

Mike arrived in fifteen minutes and we hurried out. Jeff Davis was in a patrol car across the street and another one was right out front. I didn't recognize the policemen in that car, and when are there two to a car, I asked Mike.

He pulled me to the ground as a bullet whizzed past us. The car sped off and Jeff made a quick U-turn to follow him. His chase was on.

Mike asked if I was okay, and I grunted, "You need to lose weight." He laughed, rolled over, and helped me up. "I hope Jeff catches those ass-wipes."

Mike said, "That is a big affirmative." Mike took a hold of my arm and quickly headed me back inside and said pack a bag.

I looked at him as if he had lost his mind. He said, "Do it. You aren't staying here." There was a lot of authority in his voice. You don't argue with Mike, so I did as I was told. The way I looked at it I didn't have anything here to eat anyway. I might as well go to a place that is stocked with food. If you haven't noticed, I like to be alive and eat.

Mike drove to the station, always looking at each cross street and over his shoulder. I was doing the same thing. When we entered, Jim was there waiting. He said, "What in the hell is going on?" I told him about the call and Mike coming to the rescue. I asked if he had heard from Jeff. "And how in the world did those jerks get one of our cars?"

He said Jeff lost them in the Central District, but there was already a BOLO out for the patrol car. They located the officer whose car was stolen. He was at Harborview with a concussion. I was so glad he wasn't killed.

I said, "There must be bugs hidden somewhere in our places, otherwise how did they know Mike called for backup?"

Jim said he would have both of our apartments searched. "In the meantime, I want both of you staying at a safe house." I said that was okay with me as long as there was food. They both snickered, food again. Well, I still haven't had breakfast and I'm starving. Mike told one of the officers to go down to Starbucks and get Amy a big breakfast. Jim said, "Get the receipt. This one is on us."

After I ate, we headed to the interrogation room where Mr. Dumb Shit was waiting. He glared at us and demanded why he had been waiting so long to talk with someone and where his attorney was. We said, "The attorney is coming, and we will interview you when he gets here."

It took another ten minutes before Ms. Miles arrived. Mr. Wilde blew up when a woman walked in. He demanded to have his attorney. Well, I can see he was still his obnoxious self, I thought.

Ms. Miles smiled and said, "No one else wanted to take your case, even your own attorney." She would gladly leave if that is what he wanted. It wasn't her decision to defend him; it was her un-luck of the draw. Mr. Wilde was really angry and shouted, "I'll defend myself. You won't be needed." She said thank you and left.

I asked, "Then you are waiving your rights to an attorney?" He said yes. "You need to sign this waiver then."

This was going to be fun. No attorney present and a very stupid person was sitting in front of us. Mike began with telling him we were recording the session. He grunted. "Let's start with why you went into the drug business, Brad."

"I'm Mr. Wilde to you," he said.

"Okay. Mr. Wilde, why did you go into the drug business?" He was silent. I told him his silence was not getting us anywhere but answering the question would get us out of here much quicker.

He begrudgingly said he was approached by Mr. Douglas at one of his designer parties. Craig said if he didn't go along with his plans, he would do something bad to his family. Trying to get out of dealing with drugs, I said I didn't want to and said I had no idea how any of that would work anyway. Craig said, 'Don't worry about that. I'll have someone come in to help you solve any of the problems.' I was told drug smuggling isn't rocket science. You export shoes and import materials. That's how it works. The drugs are in those shipments."

I asked, "When did this happen?"

"It was a couple of years ago."

"Did anyone see you talking with Mr. Douglas?"

He thought Rita and maybe the photographer saw them.

Oh no, not Duncan, I thought.

"We can question Rita to confirm you were talking with Craig," Mike said.

He said, "Go ahead. See if she can remember two years ago. You might get lucky."

I asked for the name of the photographer, hoping it wasn't Duncan.

He said it was the Royal Photography Studios, and he didn't remember the woman's name. "She wasn't any good anyhow, so why should I remember her name?"

I silently blew a sign of relief that is wasn't Duncan.

Mike said, "Now that we've established your connection to the drug trade, how does Mr. Douglas know we are the detectives investigating your case?"

Mr. Wilde said with a wide-eyed expression, "I don't know what you are talking about."

"Well, evidentially someone has talked with him because he tried to have Officer Wright killed this morning."

Mr. Wilde laughed and said, "I would like to have seen that."

Mike slammed his fist down on the table so hard it made it jump and shouted, "That is enough. You know this might connect you to being an accomplice in a murder attempt."

That sobered him up. He said he had no idea how Craig found out unless it was Susan.

Now Ms. Hastings reenters the picture. I asked how she fit into all of this. Mr. Wilde said he didn't know at the time he hired her that she is Craig Douglas's daughter. She was married, so her last name is different.

Mike asked, "Do you know where she could be hiding?"

"My guess would be at her father's compound in Medina. It is heavily guarded with a huge fence around it. There are cameras, movement sensors, and men located about the property."

"I thought Mr. Douglas lived in Magnolia," I said.

"He does sometimes, but most of the time he is in Medina. The house isn't listed in his name, so it is a perfect hideaway for him."

I said, "Do you know what name he used for that home?"

"No," he said.

Mike asked if he was aware that Victoria was going to be murdered. "No," he said quickly. "I wouldn't agree to anything like that."

I asked if he was aware that Rita was beaten to a pulp and then left to die in the snow. Again, he said no. I said, "Why were you at Moe's cabin?"

He replied, "I got a call from Moe, and he told me to meet at his cabin early the next morning. I thought it was to figure out how to get rid of the drugs and close down the operation. But when I got there, I was quickly blindsided and beat soundly. Both Andy and I were sure we were going to be killed. And we probably would have if you all hadn't shown up. Moe was the one who wanted to shoot our way out. He didn't have any idea how many police there were. Once he heard all the shots being fired, he knew we were done."

We were considering all of his answers when he asked how his family was doing. I said, "You should call and ask for yourself." He said he tried to call his wife, but she wouldn't talk to him. He asked me to call her and tell her he was sorry for all he did. I said I would but telling her probably wouldn't make much difference. He said, "Can you at least explain that I was trying to protect them?"

I said, "I'll let her know that, but I'm sure your womanizing ways won't sway her opinion of you much."

"What will she and the boys do without me?" he lamented.

"Well, since she is listed as a co-owner of the company, she will pick up the pieces and make a better life for herself and the boys. At least you did that right." With that, I got up and left.

Mike followed quickly behind and said, "Nice job. I was dying to say exactly what you said."

Jim and Steve, the FBI agent, came out of the room next to us and said, "Excellent job."

Steve said, "We now have enough evidence to get Douglas and Wilde indicted for drug trafficking."

I added we didn't get the name of the owner for the house in Medina. Steve said that won't be a problem. "I know the chief of police in Median. I'll call Charlie and ask him to search the area for a location fitting the description Mr. Wilde gave. There couldn't be too many houses surrounded by a high fence with cameras and guards roaming the grounds. They also have police boats since Medina is on Lake Washington. If I know Charlie, he will use all his resources to get them out of his town."

I said, "I'm glad you have what you need. Could you do us a favor when you get them? Please turn Susan Hastings over to us if you find her there." Steve agreed. He added, "If she isn't there, we will get the information for her whereabouts out of Mr. Douglas."

I said, "You sound really confident about that."

He smiled and said, "We have our ways." I thought, I'm sure you do.

Mike and I went back to the squad room. I feel there are details still missing. "I'm not sure why, but something is nagging at me," I said.

Mike nodded and said, "Then we should go over what info we have and see what piece or pieces are missing."

I agreed and said, "We have confessions from Moe, Andy, and Mr. Wilde. We know about Rita hiring Moe to off her two husbands. That looks like a slam dunk. Also, the prostitution scam was both he and Rita's doing. Mr. Douglas got Mr. Wilde involved in the drug trade. Moe got Andy to sell drugs at the U of W. That leaves Duncan Olson."

CHAPTER TWELVE

....

What Was Duncan Olson's Part?

"WHAT'S BOTHERING ME IS how Duncan Olson is connected in the scheme of things. He told us a friend asked him to rent Andy a room. He charged Andy a nominal amount of rent because he didn't have to worry about money. Then a client got him the photo shoot assignments at TWC. He lives in a very exclusive building. I know the rent is pretty high. How does he pay for it and all his expensive equipment? He was at TWC several times, so you would think he had to be suspicious of what was going on. Especially since Victoria asked him to pay for sexual favors."

Mike stared at me for a second and said, "Those are some really good questions coming from someone who was drooling the whole time we were there."

I smacked him on the arm and said, "A woman can appreciate a good-looking man, can't she? And I wasn't drooling, just blushing a lot. I wouldn't let the fact that he was a hunk interfere with a case I'm working on. And I don't let you distract me, so there."

"Oh, so you think I'm a good-looking hunk?" he said with a wicked smile.

"Oh brother, I can't win in this conversation," I said and went to get a cup of coffee. My need to get away quickly was because I was blushing again. Damn it. Mike was smiling and watching me the whole time. I could feel it.

When I got back, I was carrying a cup of coffee for him too. He said thanks and was still smiling. I reminded him we had work to do and to quit smiling he was making me nervous. He just laughed and took a drink from the cup of coffee.

"Well," he said, "I was thinking we can visit Mr. Olson again as he did indicate you were welcome anytime."

"Stop it," I said but knew he had seen Duncan looking at me. "I think it would be better if you went on your own."

He said, "Over my dead body."

I replied, "That can be arranged." His mouth fell open. I said, "Just kidding, though it is tempting at this moment." He laughed really hard and that brought Jim out of his office.

"What is going on out here?" he asked. We sobered up right away and said we were trying to wrap up one more concern.

We explained the concerns regarding Duncan Olson. Jim said, "You have some valid points. I think you need to talk with him again. Especially after what you just told me."

"I am curious about the friend and the client too," I said. "I really want to know who they are. If we know then, it will clear up most of the concerns."

"Ask the hard questions you brought up just now. They are worth looking into."

I dialed his number but Duncan didn't answer. I left a message on his answering machine saying we have a few loose ends to tie up and need to talk with him. When I was hanging up, Jim came out and told us the safe house was ready and where it was. He left and went back to his office.

We need to stop and get some food on the way to the Queen Anne location I said, "There is a QFC off of Mercer Street near the Seattle Center." Mike answered that we could just go to the hole-in-the-wall and eat.

Jim called out, "No you are too visible there. There are too many windows facing the street. We have an unmarked car ready for you to drive to the house. Your cars are to be kept in the garage. We found bugs in your apartments as well as your cars. Someone really doesn't want either of you testifying at the trials. So have food delivered to the safe house. Order it from the squad room. We went to the trouble to check for bugs here as well. Better to be safe than sorry."

I felt a chill run up my spine for the second time today. I looked at Mike, and he wasn't happy with this info either. "Okay," I asked, "what do you want for dinner and breakfast?"

"Since the tab is on the department, order a couple of steaks with seasonings for them, some potatoes, salad fixings, French bread, butter, eggs, bacon, orange juice, and coffee."

I said, "No cinnamon rolls," and giggled.

He glared and said, "No. Too much sugar isn't good for you."

I asked, "Are you cooking dinner?" He said that's an affirmative. "I will make the salad," I said, "and cook breakfast. I am no good at grilling never have been. Would you like a beverage to go along with the steaks?" I asked.

"I would, but we better make it milk," he said.

I called the QFC and asked if they delivered. The man answering said if it was close by and the total was over twenty-five dollars plus there was a delivery charge of five dollars. I said get a pencil ready and I started down the list. Mike said, "Make sure the steaks are T-bones." I nodded and added, "Make sure the stakes are T-bones," and finished by giving him the address and payment info. I asked what time he thought the delivery would be. He said in about twenty minutes. I thanked him and told Mike, "We better get a move on it or the food will arrive before us."

We parked the car in the connected garage and entered the house. There were two bedrooms, thank God, but only one bathroom. The kitchen had all the utensils we needed as well as an eating area. The living room wasn't very large, but there was a television. The decor was nothing to write home about, but it was warm and clean. I still didn't feel very safe. I went around closing all the curtains and making double sure the locks were set. Jim told us before we left to use our cells if there was a problem. He said, "Don't use the phone in the house." He also said there would be patrol cars going by the house often.

After I put my suitcase in one of the bedrooms, I went to the kitchen to help with dinner. Mike had the potatoes baking and was seasoning the steaks. He asked, "Do you know how to fix French bread?"

I glared and said, "Yes, I do cook, but grilling isn't my forte as I said before." I went to work on the bread and salad. I was starving, but it would be about forty minutes until dinner was ready. To keep my mind off my stomach, I went into the living room and turned on the TV. There was a special news alert being aired. Someone leaked the fact there were arrests made in the murder of Victoria Clump.

Mike poked his head out of the kitchen and said, "Who in the hell leaked that info?"

"How should I know? I'm as surprised as you are. To our knowledge, no one in the department was given permission to give that information to any reporter. Well, we now know for certain there is a leak at our station. Jim will be furious," I said. "I wouldn't want to be that person for love nor money. When he finds out who the dumb shit is, they won't be employed for long."

Mike reminded me that the same person could know where this safe house is. I got real close to him and whispered, "Do you know how to check the place for bugs?" He shook his head no. I whispered again, "Do you think we can go to the bathroom and talk?" He nodded and I said in a normal voice, "I have to use the bathroom," and walked in there. Mike followed quietly. I checked behind the toilet, mirror, towel bars under the sink, and around the tub. Mike was looking everything over too. We decided it was safe to talk. He suggested we keep the lights on all night and take shifts sleeping. I was in favor of that. We both agreed to keep a normal conversation going while we are in the rest of the house.

I asked if he thought the garage was bugged. He said he would check. "Could one of our patrol cars be hijacked again and used against us?" I asked.

He replied that was a possibility. He said, "After dinner, I will go to the garage and check it out. While I'm there, if it is safe, I'll call the lieutenant. He is the only one I can trust now."

I agreed. I flushed the toilet, ran the sink water, and opened the door. I walked normally and Mike quietly walked back to the kitchen. I called from the living room, "Is dinner ready? I'm starving."

Mike yelled back, "I'm just starting the steaks. How do you like yours?"

I called back, "I want mine medium rare, thank you," as I walked back into the kitchen.

"That's my girl," he said. "We should be eating in about six minutes. Please get the table set and put the bread in the oven."

I said, "Slave driver." He laughed even though we were glancing nervously about all the time. I asked, "Do you usually leave the porch light on at home?"

He said, "Yes, just in case I have a friend dropping by."

I said, "Okay, I'll turn it on then."

We ate dinner quietly as we were both extremely hungry. When I finished, I said, "I don't think I could eat another bite," and meant it.

Mike looked at me with a strange expression and said, "I'm glad since there isn't anything else left on the table."

"I was hungry and everything tasted great," I said. "I'll clean up since you cooked. Go watch a ball game or something."

He asked, "Are you sure you don't want me to dry the dishes?"

I laughed and said, "My mother taught me well. I can handle this." Then I whispered, "Look out the front window please. I will check this side of the house."

He gave me a thumbs-up and said, "Well, if you don't want help, I'll find something to watch."

I ran the water in the sink while peeking out the window, but all I could see was part of the garage. Why do they build a garage in front of a kitchen window? Then it dawned on me the garage must have been added at a later date. With the dishes done, I said, "I'm going to put my pajamas on and get comfortable." I went into the bedroom and peeked out the back of the house. There was a full moon out and with snow on the ground it was easy to see there wasn't anyone lurking there. I quickly changed but made sure my gun was hidden in the waist of my pajama bottom and under my bathrobe.

Mike asked me when I came back into the living room if I always wore pajamas with a big smile on his face. I joked back, "Wouldn't you want to know."

He said, "Maybe I'll find out one of these days."

I blushed at that comment because I knew he wasn't joking anymore. To change the subject, I asked, "What are you watching?"

He had an old program playing that happened to be one of my favorites. "I love *Hogan's Heroes*," I said. He smiled and said, "Me too. There aren't too many programs now that I really care for. I have a few but they aren't on at this time."

At that moment, we heard some bullets striking the front of the house. We both hit the deck and waited to hear footsteps coming up on the porch. We didn't have to wait long. They ran on to the porch and began to kick in the door. Both Mike and I were on our knees firing at the same time. We heard a thump, a scream, and heard someone running back to a car. There was a roar of an engine and tires squealing. Then silence. I was calling Jim while Mike was checking the porch area. I told Jim what just happened, and he said there was a patrol car already on the way. A neighbor called 911 reporting shots being fired. Mike yelled, "We got one and he is still breathing."

I said, "Put in a call for an ambulance while you are at it. We got one that is still breathing."

Jim said, "You've got it, and I'm on my way too." He hung up and I went to see who the injured person was.

We drug him into the living room to get a better look. I shut the door as best I could. It was still intact, but the hinges were loose and there were several bullet holes in it. I said, "I think I've seen this guy before."

Mike said, "You did. He was at TWC the day we took Mr. Wilde back to his office. I saw him too. It was while we were with Mr. Wilde in his office. I got a glance at him through the side window right before we left. He looked at us too intently."

A light came on. I remembered he was still in the hallway outside Mr. Wilde's office when we left. Yup, that was him. He must have been listening to our little chat. "Is that why we are now in harm's way?" I asked.

"That probably is how Mr. Douglas's crew or gang, whatever you want to call them, knew about us," Mike replied. "I'm sure he had people stationed there to keep an eye on the drug business."

Just then, the ambulance, Jim, and a squad car arrived. An officer accompanied the injured scumbag to the hospital. Harborview was going to be full of patients from this case. Mike told the officer in the squad car which direction the shooters took off in. They headed out in the direction of the getaway car. The neighbor gave the 911 operator a description of the car while he was still on the line. It was passed on to all units.

Jim looked at me in a strange way and said, "Amy, get dressed. You are showing us a little too much skin."

I looked down and my top was up and the bottoms were hanging on my hips. "Yikes!" I yelled and ran to the bedroom. "I must have done that when I was pulling my gun out of my pajama bottom," I shouted. I was getting dressed because I was sure we wouldn't be staying here.

When they got done laughing at me, Jim yelled, "You are not staying here another minute."

"I figured that one out already," I yelled back. On my way to the living room, I asked where are we going.

He answered, "To my place. No one will know where you are but me." I felt relieved. Jim and Mike had gathered what evidence there was at the front of the house while I packed and got all of our food from the refrigerator.

Mike said that was a good idea grabbing the food. "We don't want the lieutenant to go broke feeding you."

I scowled and said, "I was hungry, so sue me. If you would stop sometime during the day to grab lunch I wouldn't be so hungry at night." He just laughed and Jim smiled broadly.

We followed Jim to his house with Jeff bringing up the rear. When we arrived, I felt much safer! Monica was so nice to let us stay there. Jim took our car and had Jeff follow him to the garage. He then took out a different unmarked car for us to use in the morning. By the time he got back home, we were all huddled in the family room by a blazing fire. My only concern was the safety of Jim's family.

He said, "Don't worry. This house was built to be safe."

We were told to head upstairs and select any bedroom we wanted. Monica added their girls were away at school so we had three rooms to pick from. The she told Mike he might want the guest room as it wasn't so girly. He nodded and said okay although I probably wouldn't see what the room looked like anyway, I'm so tired. It was after midnight and we were all beat.

The next morning, I was in the bathroom when I heard a knock. I said, "I'll be out in a minute."

Mike said, "He wouldn't mind sharing it with me."

I said, "In your dreams." When I got out, he was leaning against the wall and said, "You're no fun. And furthermore, I lost a lot of sleep thinking of how cute you were in your pajamas." I punched him and blushed. He said, "Next time you put your gun inside your pajama pants, make sure they stay up when you pull your gun out. You made my heart skip a lot of beats when I looked at you after Jim said get some clothes on."

I answered back, "I don't look that bad, and it was almost the same as wearing a bikini."

He grinned and said, "I'll be the judge of that."

"You are incorrigible," I said and stomped off down the hallway.

Downstairs in the kitchen, I asked Monica if I could help make the breakfast. She said it was all ready. Sit down and dig in. There were eggs, bacon, hash browns. and toast. She thanked me for bringing the extra food. I said well it would have gone to waste if we left it there. No one will be staying there for sure until it is repaired.

She poured us a cup of coffee and asked how I liked working with Jim and Mike. I said I adored working with both of them. They are very smart and help me a lot.

She said, "I see that Mike likes working with you too." I looked a little puzzled and she said, "He has always refused to work with other women in the department. He doesn't believe they are smart or good enough to work with. You must have impressed him a lot."

"I guess it is because I work hard and don't take a lot of their crap. Some of the guys in the department like to give out a lot of it." I said. She just shook her head and said that must be it.

Just about then, Mike came in and sat next to me. He dished up his breakfast and asked what we had been chatting about. I hurriedly said, "Nothing in particular." That gave me away as Monica smiled and said, "Yes, nothing in particular." I turned and blushed. I have been doing that a lot lately. I need to get myself under control yet again.

I started concentrating on my breakfast. A little later, I asked when Jim was joining us, and she said he already had breakfast and left about thirty minutes ago. Mike just finished and said, "I need to brush my teeth and then we can head out." I needed to do that too, but I stayed and helped Monica clean up the dishes and put the leftovers away.

Before I started to go upstairs, she said, "You can't do much better than to have Mike in your life."

I said, "You are probably right about that, but right now, we need to close this case up tight."

"Yes, but think about what I just said. He thinks the world of you."

I guess I didn't see that coming but I kind of had a hunch he liked me. He was growing on me too. I remembered what he said about finding the right man and the *wow* hit me.

I went upstairs and got my toothbrush and headed into the bathroom. I could hear Mike singing in the bedroom from across the hall. He had a great voice. I liked the song he was singing too. I finished in the bathroom and got my purse. We met in the hall, and I said, "Not a bad voice you have, big guy."

He told me he sang in the choir at church, also in school choirs and with other groups in college. It had been awhile since he felt like singing but almost getting killed makes you want to live and be happy. He added, "Singing makes me happy."

"It makes me happy too, and I like to hear you, so keep it up," I said.

We thanked Monica and said, "We'll see you this evening." I asked, "Is there something you want us to pick up for dinner?"

"No," she replied. "I have everything under control. Raising three girls makes you ready for anything." We said goodbye and left.

We drove back to the station the long way around. We wanted to make sure no one was following us. We parked the car and headed for the elevator. Someone yelled. "Look out," and we hit the deck. Benny came running over and said, "Are both of you all right? I'm really sorry to have scared you, but a guy almost hit another car and I was yelling at him. I really didn't mean to scare you."

We got up, dusted ourselves off, and said, "We have had a couple of rough days." He asked if we needed him to do anything for us. I asked him to keep a close watch on the car we just drove in. He said he would, and we knew he meant it. Mike and I always treated Benny with respect. Not all the cops did. That is why he would do what we asked. That is called mutual respect. We need a lot more of that in our society.

We got on the elevator and headed to our floor. Jim was in his office talking with Carl. We assumed he had been talking with each person separately for a while now. Shawn said, "You guys are late, and it is probably a good thing. Jim is mad as hell."

We said we noticed Carl was in the hot seat now. We didn't want anyone to know we knew what it was about, so we asked why. Shawn said someone has a big mouth in the department and looked at me. Mike looked at Shawn and said with a tight lip, "It wasn't Amy. We've been working this case and haven't been out of each other's sight long enough to call anyone." Shawn gave us a look and said something off-colored.

Before Mike could respond, I squared off in front of him and said, "Knock it off. Be a little more professional, not a pig." He took offense to that and said so. I said, "Well, I took offense to what you said about me and Mike." Jim had his door open and must have heard what Shawn said. He called him to come in to his office. Jim didn't look happy and neither did Shawn.

We went to our desks and checked our phone messages. There wasn't a call back from Duncan. Mike looked up as I was about to ask if he had heard from him. Neither of us had received a return call. I told Mike I was getting a bad feeling that Duncan was tied up in all of this somehow.

I remembered him saying he had a suburban, so I checked with DOL to get the license number, color, and year of the vehicle. I got off the phone with the info and asked Mike if he thought I should put out a BOLO on it. He said, "Why don't we go to his place first?"

I asked, "What if he is involved, and someone is parked outside waiting for us to show up?"

"Good question," he said. "We can drive up there but wait a couple of blocks away. Maybe we can have someone drive by to see if his truck is there. They can go around the block a couple of times to see if someone is hanging around. If no one is in sight, they can call us and we will go ring the bell." It sounds like a solid plan to me.

We asked dispatch to call patrol officers who were patrolling that district. When he responded, we asked if he would do us a favor and told him what we wanted done.

He said it would be a piece of cake. I gave him my cell number so he could contact us. We didn't want to use our car radio as an added precaution. Shawn came out looking like he had been run over by a semi and told us he was sorry for his actions and then stomped off to his desk. We told Jim what we were doing, and he said to tell the patrol office to stay there until we come out. We said we would and left.

It looked like Duncan was home as his truck was there. Mike and I didn't know what we were going to find, but this had to be done. We knocked at his door and there wasn't an answer. I listened and thought I could hear music playing inside. Mike knocked again but harder, and the door swung open a little. Mike pushed it open a little wider with his knuckles and announced, "It is the Seattle Police. May we come in?" No response, so we went in with guns raised. The place was a shamble, and we found Duncan laying in a pool of blood. He was dead.

We called for forensics to come over right away. We called the patrol officer to get to the front door and stop anyone from coming or going except for the forensics team. This was a crime scene. Mike said, "I'm sorry," and I said, "I'm okay. I didn't know him. I just thought he was cute. Men look at women all the time without much thought can't a woman do the same." He nodded and said, "But finding a dead body is not pleasant."

It was my turn to say I'm sorry. This is not what I expected when we entered. We waited until the forensic team came in to do their thing. Rhonda, another forensic doc, came in with Lester and some other guys in uniform that I didn't know. Mike knew them and said, "How you boys been?" They said, "Still kicking," and went to work.

"We need to find evidence as to why he was murdered," I said.

Mike agreed. He said, "Wait here and I'll check out the rest of the apartment."

I said, "Oh no, you aren't going by yourself. This place is too big and someone can still be hiding. You might not see them until it's too late. I'll have your back." He smiled and off we went.

We went back to the bedrooms first. I opened the door to what we thought was Duncan's room. It was in shambles. Someone had torn all the clothes off the hangers and just left them on the floor. They had turned over the mattress and torn it to shreds. The drawers were pulled out, emptied, and left turned over on the floor. It was a disaster. Mike shook his head and said, "We won't find anything in here." There might be prints so he yelled for Lester to print it.

One look at it and Lester said, "Can someone bring me dinner?" We laughed but knew it was a daunting task for him. The next room was slightly messed up. Mattress moved, drawers pulled out, but still in the dresser. This one was only a guest room. I had a hunch and pulled out each drawer all the way. The dresser drawers in his bedroom were completely overturned and emptied out onto the floor. I guess they didn't think to do the same to these. The bottom drawer had an envelope taped on the underside. I put the drawer on the bed. The first thing we saw was a note. It stated, "Hopefully you will find this packet if I am dead."

Mike and I started removing the tape carefully. We didn't want anything ruined. Oh my god, there were photographs of Susan and Mr. Douglas. It was taken at night in Mr. Wilde's office, and it looked like they were looking for something. The last picture was blurry as if Duncan took off running. "I was trying to get more on them, but

I'm sure they saw me taking this last picture" was written on it. These might have been taken during a party or photo shoot otherwise why would he be there.

At the bottom of the stack of pictures was a note saying, "These people are responsible for my father's death. I have a safety deposit box at Seattle First Savings and Loan on Fourth Avenue with evidence to prove it. The key is in the guest bathroom under the sink in a box of Kleenex."

I said, "Didn't we find pictures, documents, and a note at Victoria's place? Maybe Andy asked Duncan for his help," I said.

"Yah, he might have and Duncan agreed because he wanted them, meaning Douglas and Hastings, tied into the whole mess as well as connecting them to his dad's murder," Mike said. We need to see what info is in the safety deposit box. If it is really what Duncan thought it was, then it could tie those two into his death as well. After all, Duncan gave up his life to get justice for his father."

"I wouldn't be surprised if Moe was responsible for this death as well. That creepy weasel. Let's go get that key." We went across the hallway to the bathroom. It was the closest one to this bedroom. Mike got down on his knees and started pulling stuff out. There was a bunch of Kleenex boxes. He pulled the bottom one out. It had been opened. He pulled out about half the box of tissues before he had the key. We were on our feet jumping up and down screaming. Lester came running with a bat in his hand as he thought we were being attacked and said, "Thanks for scaring the hell out of me."

We both said, "We found some very important evidence. Sorry we scared you." I then asked, "What's with the bat?"

He said, "It was under the bed and was the only available weapon I could get my hands on."

I said, "Well done," and smiled. Lester smiled back.

Mike told him, "In the bedroom across from here are pictures and a note on the bed that needs to be bagged with care and marked very important. You will need a medium-sized evidence bag." Lester nodded and went directly down the hall to get it. We watched him coming quickly back to the bedroom, and he carefully pick up the packet along with the envelope and placed them in the evidence bag and labeled it "very important" in capital letters. He took it out and placed it in a plastic tub with other items that were already bagged and labeled. He closed the tub and sealed it. He told Rhonda he had all the evidence he needed, and she said she was done too.

The coroner's van had arrived while we were in the bathroom. Rhonda's helper had taken Duncan's body to the morgue so Ben could do the autopsy. Rhonda told us he was getting tired of the bodies stacking up in this case. She yelled to us, "Solve this for crying out loud."

Mike and I yelled back, "We are trying, but there are so many twists and turns we are getting dizzy." Rhonda said Ben had filled her in on all that was going on, and she agreed that we had our hands full.

We locked up the apartment, and officers placed yellow tape on the door so no one could enter without us knowing. We thanked everyone for their help and started for the car. Mike put his hand out to stop me from getting in. He immediately raised the hood, looked all around the engine compartment, then got down on his hands and knees and looked at the undercarriage. He said it looks clean and got in his side. I hesitated for a second but decided it might be safer inside than out. At least there was some metal around us. He started the engine and nothing happened. I let out my breath. I wasn't even aware that I had been holding it. Mike smiled and said, "We are going straight to the bank. Let Jim know that we will be back soon."

I asked, "Why so cryptic a message?"

"He might not be in his office and someone could hear the message you are leaving."

"You are so right." I called, and luckily, he was there. I told him what we found. He already heard about the murder. He let me know that the person leaking all the info was Carl, and he was no longer there. Charges have been brought up against him for obstruction of justice.

I was surprised. I would never have thought in a million years that Carl would be the one responsible for any wrongdoing. He could have gotten us killed. I asked Jim if he said who he was giving the info to. No, he wasn't forthcoming with names. Hence the charges. I felt bad for his family but not for him. I passed on the details of my conversation with Jim. Mike was as surprised as me.

We got to the bank and showed our badges and ID to the bank manager. We requested to see Duncan's lock box. We had pictures of Duncan laying on the floor. He grimaced when he looked at the photo. He went to get the other key. Once both keys had been inserted, he turned to go. I asked him if he would wait outside the room. He asked why and I said, "In case someone comes down here, we want to know." He hesitated but said he would be our lookout. We smiled and thanked him.

Mike placed the box on the table. It held photos of an automobile that was unrecognizable. There was a death certificate with the name Harold Olson. We didn't need to read further. The newspaper articles stated it was a hit and run by a large box truck. There was one witness, a Mary Winters. Another article with a later date said she had disappeared soon after the accident happened. Oh, brother another one. It looked like Duncan took pictures of the scene as they were there too. One in particular had a big red circle around a group of people. In the group were Susan, Mr. Douglas, and Moe. They were all smiling, not something people usually do at a horrible accident scene.

I'm sure this photo put Duncan on the hunt to find out who they were. Maybe it wasn't pure luck he had been hired to do photo shoots and take pictures of parties at TWC. The last piece of evidence was a logbook with dates, names, locations, and what had taken place at each event. He had been very through, but it had cost him everything in the end.

CHAPTER THIRTEEN

....

Can We Now Wrap This Case Up?

WHEN WE GOT TO the station, I researched Harold Olson to find out more about him and his family. Mr. Olson had been a crab fisherman and accumulated a large fortune doing it. It said he also made smart investments. Then an article I found concerning his death said he had a wife, Martha; a son, Duncan; a daughter, Dorothy; and an adopted child named Ruby. She was the daughter of a crabber who lost his life in the Bering Sea.

Could this be the Ruby working at TWC? If so, that would explain why she knew so much about Rita. She was searching for information for Duncan. There was an address for Mrs. Olson. The home was located in the Blue Ridge district of Seattle, another awesome area. Some of the houses are located on the shores of Puget Sound. They are also very expensive but older. A lot of retired fishermen live there. Fishermen are a tight-knit group. A lot of the them live in Ballard. Blue Ridge is a part of the Ballard area. There are lot of Norwegian people there. I said I found the widow of Mr. Harold Olson.

We need to let her know of her son's death. I think we might find Ruby there too. Mike had a question mark written all over his face. I said Duncan had a sister who was adopted. Her name is Ruby. That brought him to attention. She was probably the friend who

Duncan said recommended him to Mr. Wilde. After all, they didn't look alike. I'm not sure if their last names are the same. She could have married and divorced her husband. Or being raised in the fishing community, it wasn't a stretch in thinking he was a crabber and lost his life doing that.

We told Jim about my findings and that we were going out to deliver the sad news. We also wanted to see if Ruby was who we thought she might be. He said, "Be careful, and why don't you change cars again just to be on the safe side?" We agreed and went to the garage and asked Benny for a different vehicle. He had one for us right away.

We drove north to Blue Ridge and found Mrs. Olson's home. It was a very nice older colonial painted white with black shutters. We weren't sure if she would be home, but we had to take a chance. We pulled up in front and walked to the door. It opened without us having to knock. There stood Ruby. She had an anguished look on her face. I think she knew why we were here.

We asked if we could come in. She escorted us into the living room. Mrs. Olson was sitting in a wingback chair looking out at the sound. Ruby said, "Mother, I think you should come sit by me. There are some people here that I know and I want you to meet them." She turned and walked stiffly over to us and sat down.

Mike introduced us and said, "I hate to be the bearer of bad news, but we found your son and he is dead." Both Ruby and Mrs. Olson gasped and started crying. Ruby got herself under control first and asked what happened. I said, "We went to ask him some questions to wrap up loose ends. We found the door ajar and saw him lying in the living room. We searched the apartment and found some information he had been compiling against Mr. Douglas, Susan Hastings, and Moe. Ruby, I'm sure you are aware of what we found." She nodded.

Mrs. Olson finally spoke up, "I told him to leave it alone. I was sure it would end badly. These people have no hearts. I didn't want any of my children to die unnecessarily. That is why I wouldn't let Duncan go crabbing. I worried every season I wouldn't get Harold back alive. When he retired, I was so happy! Then to have someone

115

run him down in his car like he didn't matter. He didn't deserve that. He was a very good man." With that, she started to cry softly again. Ruby went and put her arm around her mother.

She looked up and said, "We suspected it was a case of mistaken identity. Poppa's Volvo might have fit the description of someone else's car. Duncan felt it too and couldn't let it go. He wanted the people responsible to pay for taking Poppa's life. My birth father worked for Poppa, and when he was lost in the Bering Sea, Poppa wouldn't let anyone take me. He said he was responsible, and he would love and care for me as if he was my own father. He kept his promise. All of us wanted justice, even Dorothy. She doesn't live in the state, but while she was here for the funeral, she said she would do all she could to help. Duncan showed her the picture he had taken at the accident site with the three circled in red. She said she would find out who they were. She found out they were Mr. Douglas and Susan Hastings. Dorothy is a reporter and does a lot of research. Moe was a little harder to find. She also found a link between Mr. Douglas and Mr. Wilde.

"I told Duncan I would go to work there and get as much information as I could. He didn't want me to do it at first, but I convinced him. I did get a lot of evidence. It is still at TWC. I found a great hiding place in the factory. Some of the ladies didn't like Mr. Wilde and were happy to hide it. He always treated them like they were dirt and that didn't sit well with them."

I got a call from Jim. I explained I need to answer this right away and walked back to the entryway. Jim said the Feds got Mr. Douglas and Susan Hastings in custody. It is the best news we could ever hope to get.

When I returned, I was smiling and said, "You can rest easy as the FBI just took Mr. Douglas and Susan Hastings into custody." Ruby and Mrs. Olson beamed. I added, "Moe, Andy, and Mr. Wilde are already in jail."

Ruby had tears running down her checks. "Don't worry, these are tears of joy," she said. "You don't have any idea what they all have put us through."

I said, "We have an inkling of what it was like." Mike nodded.

I asked if it was alright if we retrieved the information she had TWC. She said, "I'll go with you to get it. Just wait a minute." She went over to the intercom and said, "Molly, will you please come down an sit with mother while I go out for a while?" She replied she would be right there.

Ruby asked if she could follow us as she wanted to let the TWC ladies know they were safe now. I asked, "Where are they?"

She answered, "We put them up at the Edgewater." I was so pleased that she knew where they were so I told her that. "My brother didn't want them to be harmed because of what we were doing. He was a great guy, and we will miss him greatly," she said. There were tears in her eyes again, and she had to wipe them away.

She asked as we were walking out where Duncan's body was. I told her because of the way we found him, there had to be an autopsy. She said, "Can I call the morgue and have the mortuary pick him up?" I gave her the number to call.

I said, "Would you let us know when and where the funeral will be held? We would like to honor him by being there."

She nodded and grabbed my hand. Mike took both our hands in his and said, "We shouldn't stay out in the open too long, so let's hurry to the car. When we get to it, we will drive away without warming it up. Do you have a car that wouldn't be recognizable if someone is still watching you?"

She opened the garage to house door and said she would drive the car she got for graduation. It was an old Mustang and it was a beauty. Mike was drooling over it.

She said, "I keep it purring like a kitten, and I only drive it on special occasions. I never drove it to work. My other car is at my apartment, so no one will recognize this one. No one can connect me to this address either as my married name is Wilson. That is the name I used when I rented the apartment. I divorced soon after my father died. My husband was an asshole anyway." With that, she got in the car. She pushed the garage door opener, backed out, and left.

We hustled out to our car to keep up with her. Mike said, "I would rather have driven that beautiful piece of work. It is something

I've always wanted." I agreed as I wanted to drive it too. I love fast cars and that one was built to race.

We arrived at TWC after hours, and Ruby unlocked the door. We entered with our guns drawn. I hadn't noticed before, but Ruby had a .38 special in her hand. She looked at me, smiled, and said, "I have a permit to carry a concealed weapon. I've been shooting since I was twelve years old, so don't worry, I won't accidently shoot you."

It was okay with me. I said, "The more firepower we have, the better our chances are if we meet up with another scumbag. I don't like empty buildings anyway."

Ruby headed to the warehouse with us right on her heels. She went to the locker room. I stood outside in case someone we couldn't see was in the warehouse. Mike followed Ruby to the locker room where the evidence was. It was paddle locked, but Claire had given her the combination. The packet was still there and hadn't been tampered with. Mike put it in his jacket and said, "We better get out of here. I don't want your mother to have two funerals to plan."

Ruby said, "I'm right behind you." I brought up the rear. We reached the door to the hallway when we heard someone coming.

There was a small alcove near the door, and we all squeezed in. It was only Mr. Crane. He looked around and said, "Is anyone here? Please come out. I have the police on the way."

Mike stepped out and Mr. Crane jumped a foot in the air. He said, "I'm sorry we scared you." Mr. Crane was holding his chest and breathed a sigh of relief. He explained he had been staying to make sure no one broke in while the investigation was going on. He said, "I want Mrs. Wilde to have no trouble when she takes over."

Ruby and I had joined Mike. Ruby said, "Carl, I didn't know you knew that."

He smiled and said, "I know all sorts of things that go on here. I have worked here since I graduated high school. That was way before Mr. Wilde took over the company. His daddy was the owner and let Mr. Tightwad have it when he retired. I was really sorry he did that. Mr. Wilde's half-sister could have done a much better job."

I said, "I didn't know he had a sister."

Carl replied, "Oh yes. She works here, her name is Claire. Mr. Tightwad never claimed her because she was born by a different woman. His daddy had a wandering eye too. I met his wife once, and I can tell you I understood why he had a mistress. That woman could pickle a cucumber with one look."

"So that's why Claire was so interested in helping," I said.

Ruby was still gaping until she said, "I'm so surprised." Carl chuckled. Ruby added, "I had no idea she was related to that no-good son of a sea biscuit." She looked at me and whispered, "I don't want to swear in front of Carl. He is a true gentleman." We all agreed about Mr. Wilde being no good. Carl just stood there smiling.

"I'm beginning to believe everyone in Seattle is related in some way." Mike knew why I said that. He added if Nicole was really interested in keeping the business going, all of the workers would be happy to help her.

Ruby said, "I know I would." She was always smiling and treating all of us really well. I asked her if she knew that Sarah was Nicole's sister. She said, "You're kidding, right?"

I shook my head no. "She is and that is why she helped Victoria put files containing evidence in her car. They held important information about the drug smuggling going on here. Victoria wanted to get Mr. Wilde, Mr. Douglas, Moe, and Susan Hasting charged for the drug smuggling they were into. Sarah wanted to help when Victoria told her what was in the box. Evidently, Moe saw them and ratted them out to Mr. Douglas. If Victoria hadn't been murdered, she would have taken it to the police. They got to her before she had a chance to turn it over. Though she was smart enough to hide it in her apartment."

Ruby sadly said, "I wish Duncan and I had known she was compiling info. We would gladly have helped her. We could have provided a double whammy against those despicable people. Two people lost their lives trying to put those scumbags behind bars. That is so sad. My brother didn't have a very high opinion of Victoria, but if he had known what she was doing, I'm sure he would have changed his mind in a New York minute."

That statement made me think of Andy. I asked her if she knew if Duncan had any inkling Andy was involved. She replied she didn't think so. He never mentioned him in connection with the others. "Duncan told me he thought he was just plain not interesting. They didn't have anything in common. They never had any long talks. He would come in say hi and head for his room. Andy only shared information he wanted Duncan to know like asking Victoria to marry him. Andy was very excited about that. He really loved her, and I know Victoria was very much in love with him. Both of us wondered why."

You aren't the only one who wondered that, I thought.

Mike interrupted the conversation to say, "I think we have hung around here long enough. Let's get this evidence back to the station." I asked Ruby if she would be alright going back home by herself. Carl spoke up that he would follow her at a distance to make sure she was okay.

Ruby said, "No, I'll be fine, but thank you. I want to stop by the funeral home we use to let them know Duncan will be coming there."

Carl gasped. "Oh no, not Mr. Duncan. I really liked him. What happened?"

Ruby looked at him and said, "Duncan was my brother, and he was murdered yesterday by the scumbags we are trying to put in prison. Some of this evidence is pictures he took. He was also asking questions at photo shoots and parties that were held around here. He kept a log of the answers. One of the jerks, to put it nicely, must have seen him."

Carl crossed himself and told her how sorry he was and that he really like Mr. Duncan. "Such a good man," he said.

With that said, we all bid each other goodbye. We headed back to the station, Ruby to the funeral home, and Carl...Well, I'm not sure. He just stayed there with his head bowed. I'm sure he was saying a prayer. I'm glad he is the good man I thought he was on our first meeting. So far there haven't been too many of those around lately. At least Duncan turned out to be one of the good guys.

We pulled into the garage, and Benny said he was worried because we were gone so long. We thanked him for his concern and went upstairs. Mike took the packet out from under his jacket and dumped the contents on his desk.

Jim came and asked us, "What treasurers have you brought us now?" FBI Steve came out too.

We said, "We are not sure, but it was evidence Duncan Olson and his sister Ruby had been collecting."

Jim looked puzzled and said, "Sister? So she was the one listed in the article."

I replied, "Yes, Ruby was Duncan's adopted sister. She had a different last name because of her marriage. She told us she was the friend who got Duncan the photo gig at TWC. They were trying to get enough evidence to connect everyone to their dad's murder. Duncan's info has a picture of Mr. Douglas, Moe, and Susan laughing it up at the accident scene. He has them circled in a red pen. Laughing at a tragedy isn't normal. This wasn't just and accident. It was done on purpose. The problem is the car fit the description of who was to be kill, but it was the wrong driver."

Jim shook his head and said, "So many murders all tied in together. I've never seen any other case to match this one."

"There might be another one," I said. "There was a witness to the accident in the article. A couple of weeks later, she disappeared."

Jim let out a groan. "Not another one? We can probably wrap that one up with this case. I'm sure Douglas, Hastings, and Morella are responsible."

Steve asked, "Do you mind if I look at what you have?"

We didn't see it being a problem. I said, "There might be something in there to put another nail in Mr. Douglas's coffin, the scumbag. I was secretly hoping there would be. It would be a shame if Duncan died for nothing."

Mike had been standing there idly but started to separate the information. There were pictures again, notes, little scraps of paper with writing on them, and the logbook. I said, "Let's start with the little scraps. Sometimes those have the best information." We all picked up one.

Mine was about a meeting that took place in the warehouse between Moe and Mr. Douglas. They were talking about a drug cartel I had never heard about. I handed it to Steve. Wow was all he said and hurried to Jim's office to make a call. He dropped his note, so I grabbed it and read the three assholes, Duncan's description of the red circle, were talking about another person they wanted to have eliminated. The name was Duncan's. He knew they were planning on killing him, and he kept going. I dropped the note like it was on fire. Mike and Jim looked at me, and I said, "There is the proof we need to show how they planned to kill Duncan."

They said, "He knew?" I nodded. Jim placed it in a manila folder and marked it evidence—Duncan Olson's murder. Mike had written on another manila folder which he marked evidence—Victoria Clump's murder. The third folder was evidence—drug trade. We began filling all the folders. All this would be copied and then the originals would be given to the prosecuting attorney. The drug trade info would go to the FBI and to the DEA after we made copies for us of course.

Steve came out and said they had their office in Arizona set up a raid on the drug cartel mentioned in the note. The police in Juarez, Mexico, will assist. Mike said, "I hope the police lined up are the honest ones. You might be putting your associates in harm's way."

Steve replied, "One of the guys there has a brother who works in the Juarez police department. Juan wouldn't let his brother down."

I finished with the last note and said, "Should we start on the regular-sized notes now, or go get something to eat?" Everyone said, "Let's eat." I looked at Mike and said, "The same place?"

Steve asked, "Where is that? I've never heard of a restaurant named the Same Place." We all laughed and explained about the hole-in-the-wall we all loved to eat at.

Steve laughed and said, "I'm in and it will be my treat. The department has been working on Douglas for a couple of years, and we haven't accumulated this much information in two years as you guys have in just three days." I was beginning to like Steve. But was it only three days?

We walked over to the diner, and Vivian met us at the door. She showed us to the booth at the back, and before anyone could reach for a menu, she said the special tonight is goulash served with a salad and a roll. I raised my hand, and she knew I wanted it. Mike smiled and said me too. Steve looked puzzled but said count me in on it. Jim was the only hold out. He wanted spaghetti. He said, "You have the best spaghetti in the world. My wife just can't get it right."

I stared at him and said, "I'm going to tell Monica when we get to your house."

"She already knows," he said and grinned. "She won't even try to make it anymore."

Before Vivian left, she found out what we wanted to drink. I loved their lemonade and had it again. The others ordered coffee. I don't know how they sleep with all the caffeine they consume during the day and evening. Our meals came, and we ate like there was no tomorrow.

There wasn't a crumb left on any of the plates. Steve said, "If I had known this place existed, I would be three hundred pounds by now." Vivian came over and asked who wants desert. I raised my hand again and she said, "Coconut cream, I assume." I smiled and said. "Yes, please." Mike was shaking his head, and I reminded him that he helped me eat the last piece. He said. "In that case, Vivian, give me one to go too."

Steve was looking at me and said, "Where is she putting all of this?"

Jim said, "Don't worry, she will burn it off. We don't let her sit on her butt very long." Then the two of them also ordered pie to take. We walked out well satisfied and carrying delightful pieces of pie to eat later.

We heard the squeal of tires and ducked down behind an SUV parked in front of the diner. We had to pull Steve down as he didn't know what was going on. Jim was immediately on his cell calling for patrol cars to come to the aid of officers being fired at and gave our location.

We all got shots off before the car roared away. I was sure I hit it as I heard glass shatter, and I was aiming at the back windshield.

I was able to get the make and color of the SUV. Steve got a look at the driver and was surprised that it was an older woman. Mike got a partial license number. All of this was forwarded to the patrol cars.

We rushed back into the diner to make sure everyone inside was okay. Most of the patrons were in shock as this had never happened before. I asked Vivian if she would be okay, and she said, "I'm from Brooklyn. Do you think a little gunfire is going to scare me? No way, I've seen a lot worse," and I believed her.

A few minutes later, a call came to Jim saying they had the shooter in custody. We took off to the station to see who it was. Steve was the first to say, "Well, I'll be damned. If it isn't Mrs. Douglas. How you doing? Was it worth shooting at us?" he asked.

She just glared and said, "No, I missed," and with that the officers escorted her up to jail.

Steve turned to us and said, "Now we have the whole family in custody."

I don't know what made me do it, but I asked, "So insanity must run in the family?" It was just the right thing to say because it broke the tension we had been under. Steve and the others were laughing really hard.

"Well put," Steve finally said when he could catch a breath.

"I, for one, think we all need a good night's rest," I said.

Steve uttered, "I know I do, and I'm going home to see my wife and hopefully the kids. Then go get some me time with my wife." Jim agreed and went into his office to get his coat.

Mike said, "We will be over in a little while to get out stuff. We need to eat this pie before someone else discovers it in the fridge."

Steve said, "I'm taking mine home. I'll share it with my wife." Jim added he was doing the same.

They left and I asked Mike if we could take ours to go to. I want get our stuff then eat the pie at my apartment. I said I didn't feel safe just yet. He said you bet and went into the kitchenette to get our pies.

We thanked Monica and Jim after getting our belongings then went to the car. I was still looking over my shoulder. Mike asked if I was okay.

I answered, "I'm just not used to getting shot this many times. I would feel better if I were sure she was the only one shooting at us. I don't know, but I seem to remember there were two people in the car the first time around." Mike didn't say anything just started the car and drove a roundabout way to my apartment. We stopped at the grocery store nearby. I bought some milk and breakfast fixings for the next morning.

He followed me up to the apartment. I know he was protecting my back. He opened the door and entered first. I was looking back down the hallway when he poked his head out and said everything is okay. I quickly entered, shut, and locked the door. Mike was putting the pie on the table and had already poured the milk.

He said, "How comfortable is that couch?"

I smiled and said, "I have a spare bedroom, which you are more than welcome to use." So that was settled. I didn't have to ask him to stay; he knew how worried I was.

The pie and milk went down much smoother now. I said, "You can use the bathroom first. I'll make up the bed and clean up the kitchen." He came out when I was just putting the last dish in the cupboard. He smiled and headed into the bedroom and closed the door. I thought it would have been nice to have a hug before he went in there. Oh well, I can sleep good tonight with him here.

I was surprised that I slept like a log. Was I smelling coffee? I looked at the clock; it was 6:20. I had overslept. I jumped out of bed and ran out to the kitchen wondering how the coffee was already perking. I had completely forgotten that Mike was here. He was leaning against the counter and said, "Shouldn't you put a house coat on or something maybe not quite so inviting?"

I gasped and yelled, "I forgot you were here," while running back to the bedroom. I couldn't hide the blush on my face because I was wearing a short baby doll nightgown. I wanted to crawl under the carpet, but I didn't have one. Hardwood floors are really difficult to hide under.

I put on my housecoat, grabbed the clothes I was going to wear, and ran to the bathroom for a quick shower and got dressed. I emerged fully clothed and composed. Mike was still smiling, but there were eggs, toast, bacon, and hot coffee on the table. I sat down and said, "Sorry I overslept and didn't make the breakfast."

He just smiled and said, "Your entrance this morning made up for it." I couldn't help blushing again and whispered, "Stop it." He chuckled and kept smiling.

I didn't want to keep this conversation going, so I changed the subject. "Do you think I was being paranoid last night?"

He shook his head no. "There is the possibility Mr. Douglas hired some thugs to help his cause." That possibility didn't make me feel any better. He said, "Let's clean up, and I'll drive back to the station while you keep your eyes peeled for bad guys."

I said, "Don't try to be funny," but got busy clearing the table.

Kevin had overheard Mike talking about taking me to my apartment the night before and had spread the news. There were some awes coming from the officers in the squad room when we entered. Mike said, "Get your minds out of the gutter. Her apartment has two bedrooms. She was in one with me in the other." That only made them laugh.

I wasn't in the mood to be joked with and said, "If any of you want to join us in getting shot at, be our guests. I, for one, want to get through this case without holes in me. Got it!" That shut them up except for Kevin.

He said, "I'm sorry. We were just trying to lift your spirits."

That made me feel like a heel and I said, "I'm sorry too. This case just keeps getting bigger and bigger." With that said, we sat down and I asked, "Where do we go now?"

CHAPTER FOURTEEN

....

What You've Got to be Kidding?

MIKE HAD BEEN QUIET but looked at me and said we needed to interrogate Mr. Wilde to see if he can give us more information regarding Mr. Douglas and Susan Hastings. I shouldn't be there. "I can watch through the glass in the next room while you do the interrogation," I said.

Mike started to protest, but I said, "Yes, I'm the lead, but he has such a hatred for women I don't think he will tell us anything more if I'm there. After Mr. Crane told us about Mr. Wilde's mother, I'm sure that is the reason for his hatred."

Mike said, "You are probably right, and it might be a good idea."

After mentioning Mr. Crane's name and thinking of his first name, it got me to thinking about Carl who is no longer employed here. I asked, "Do you think we can get any information out of Carl as to who is shooting at us?" Mike said it would be worth a try. He suggested he start with Mr. Wilde first. He called the jail and requested them to bring Mr. Wilde down to the interrogation room one.

I went straight to the adjoining room and waited for Mike and Mr. Wilde. Mike was sitting when they brought Brad in. I love saying his first name because it had irritated him so much when I said it. Mike started with "You are in a whole lot of trouble and can only help yourself by telling us more of what you know." Brad just sat there staring at the ceiling. "Okay, let me start. We found all the drugs, books, and money at your business. You won't be able to say you didn't know because we have pictures and witnesses that place you with all of it. Furthermore, you were involved in forcing women to sleep with you. You were blackmailing Rita and helping Moe. You shot at police officers and resisted arrest. You confessed to the drug dealings and everything else I just mentioned. Your sister helped hide some additional evidence."

With that he turned beet red and said, "I don't have a sister. Well, on Claire's birth certificate it states that your father is her father. I guess that makes her your half-sister. You have treated her like dirt. Instead of helping her, you made her work in the factory. By rights, half of all you have is hers. You didn't give her anything except a menial job. The only thing she ever said against you was you are rude. The behavior you showed the factory and warehouse workers was totally unacceptable. That didn't sit well with her. They are all looking forward to having Nicole as their boss. Carl will suggest to Nicole that Claire be promoted to supervisor of the factory workers."

He said, "She can't do that. I own the company."

"Not anymore. Nicole has filed papers to remove your name from the company charter."

Mr. Wilde yelled, "She can't do that."

"She can and she will as the co-owner. You are now a felon and you have no rights. The only way a jury is going to take any pity on you is if you start giving us something to work with. Now is your opportunity."

Mr. Wilde just looked at him and said, "Drop dead."

I couldn't stand it anymore and stormed into the interrogation room. I said, "You are the biggest dunderhead I have ever seen." He started to get up, and I pushed him back down as the adrenaline was rushing through me. I said, "I'm not going to be bullied by you. I'm not your mother. Now don't ever disrespect detective Bowers again. Start talking or you will never see the light of day if I have anything to say about it." Mike was just beaming.

Mr. Wilde started laughing and said, "You will never make it to the courtroom."

"Oh, so you know about the target on our backs. That also means you know who put it there and who they hired to do it," I said. Mike got up and walked around to his side of the table.

Mr. Wilde got wide-eyed and said, "You can't do anything to me."

"I can," Mike said. He was towering over him. "No one here will lift a finger to help you. You are scum to them." Mr. Wilde got white as a sheet and started to sweat. "Talk," Mike said in the roughest voice I've ever heard.

Mr. Wilde said he thought it was Mr. Douglas. He knew a couple of thugs he uses but only by their first names. One was Randy and the other was Wilbur.

I asked, "Do these thugs have records?"

Mr. Wilde said, "I think so. Maybe not here, but in Texas I'm sure they do. They told me one day that they were never going back there."

Mike said, "Do you know what city they lived in?"

He thought it was Houston but wasn't sure. I asked, "Was one of them at the company while we were talking with you?"

"Wilbur was always there making sure I didn't screw Mr. Douglas. I am really afraid of these two. They would just as soon slit your throat as look at you."

"Well, is there any other information you want to share now?"

"Susan Hastings was instrumental in getting me sucked into being partners with Mr. Douglas. She was recommended to me by a Daniel Davidson when I was looking for an HR director. He is another manufacturer, I believe he makes machinery. She worked for him and had already hooked him into the drug business. His plant is down in Vancouver. I'm sure the DEA would like to shut that operation down too. That is all I really know," Mr. Wilde said.

"There is one more thing, did you know they killed Duncan Olson?"

"Hell no. What did he know?""

"Well, he knew Mr. Douglas, Susan, and Moe were instrumental in killing him and Ruby's father. They were getting information to prove that. Do you remember Ruby recommending Duncan?"

"Well, maybe, but Mr. Douglas put the final approval on his hiring."

"So maybe you weren't in on them planning his murder. That is all I wanted to find out. Mike, do you have anything else you would like to know?"

Mike shook his head no and headed out the door. I said, "Have a nice life in prison."

He yelled, "I thought you were going to help me." That is the last thing I heard out of him. Or ever wanted to hear out of him again.

Mike and I went to Jim's office and told him to call the DEA and give them Daniel Davidson's name in Vancouver. It was another drug dealer location Mr. Douglas had in place. Then we asked where we could find Carl because we wanted to ask him some questions. Jim got his address, and we were off to talk with him. Jim yelled as we were walking out to be careful. That was a given as we didn't want to get shot.

We got to Carl's house in the Wallingford district, and no one was home. A neighbor was getting into his car and we hailed him. He came over and we asked him if he knew where Carl was. He said he saw him taking a cab earlier that morning. He added it was a yellow cab.

"Do you remember the time?" I asked. He said, "Yes, it was 7:30 a.m." He explained he had just gotten the newspaper and looked at the clock when he went back into the house.

Mike asked if he got the cab number. He didn't get the number because it wasn't uncommon to see Carl taking a cab at that time of the morning although this time he had a couple of suitcases with him. "Well, there goes that lead," I said. We thanked him for his time, and he said no problem, got in his car, and drove off. I looked at Mike. We both shrugged our shoulders and got in the car to drive back to the station.

When we got back, we reported to Jim that we thought Carl had skipped town. He got on the phone to have an arrest warrant issued for Carl Moore on suspicion of aiding in multiple murder attempts.

"Now why would he be taking cab rides at the same time of the morning?" Jim said. We shook our heads as we didn't have a clue. Carl's shift started later in the day. He drove a car to work every day. I suggested getting a warrant to search his house.

Jim agreed and requested one. We waited about thirty minutes for the warrant to arrive and then it was back to Carl's house.

When we arrived, we were met by the same neighbor. He said he saw someone creeping around the house and yelled at the man, and he ran down the street. I asked how long ago was that. He thought and said it was no longer than four minutes ago. He gave us a description, and it sounded a lot like Wilbur. We asked what direction was he headed and he said east. There was a freeway entrance about eight blocks from there, so he probably had a car stashed a couple of blocks away and was already on I-5.

I asked, "Did Carl leave a key with a neighbor in case of an emergency?"

"As a matter of fact," he said, "he left one with me. I'm retired and here most of the time." We showed him the search warrant and asked him to get the key for us. We added that we didn't want to break down his front door.

He said, "What in the world is going on? For crying out loud, he is a police officer."

We didn't want to go into details and said he didn't report for work and wasn't on vacation, so something might have happened that made him afraid to stay in his house. That seemed to appease the neighbor so he got the key.

"It feels strange searching a comrade's house," I said.

Mike just looked at me and said, "Where do you want to start?"

I said, "I'll take downstairs. You can look through the bedrooms upstairs."

He asked, "Did you lock the front door?"

I said an emphatic yes. "I really don't want someone popping in unannounced." I started in the kitchen. People hid things in the freeze, so I started there. Well, Carl had a sweet tooth, almost everything was candy and ice cream. Nothing I wanted to see.

I look in the cupboards and took everything out. Nothing of interest in them. Looked in the stove and didn't find anything in there. I stopped and wondered why I looked in there. Maybe my gut was telling me to. I shrugged and went to the living room. I just started pulling all the cushions off of the couch when I heard Mike whistle. I ran upstairs and into the front bedroom; he wasn't there. I ran down the hall and found him in the bathroom.

He was sitting on the floor with a wad of cash in his hand and some drugs. I couldn't help myself and said, "Oh my god, not Carl." Mike was as shook as I was. Never in a million years would I have thought Carl was into this crap. Mike looked at me and said, "I bet this is what Wilbur was looking for."

"Is there anything else hidden? Maybe he was getting evidence," I said. Mike shook his head and got up. Now we had to find the connection between Carl and Mr. Douglas. I called Jim's cell phone and told him what we found. I said we need to contact the phone company and get a printout of all his calls for the last month or maybe longer. Mike said, "Also his bank account. There is a wad of cash that looks like about ten thousand dollars. I don't think he had time to deposit it yet."

"Oh my god" was all Jim said. After he composed himself, he said he would have all of this when we got back.

Sure enough, our fears were confirmed; he was in cahoots with the scumbags. No wonder they knew where we lived and what we drove. And to have him tell them where we would be eating made me furious. No one messes with where I eat especially the hole-in-the-wall.

I still had a hard time believing Carl would do this. Jim went into the squad room and asked if anyone was close enough to Carl to know where he might have gone to.

In order to get them to talk, he told them what had been happening. You could hear the disbelief coming from all the officers who knew Carl. They were all saying how could he do that.

Kevin spoke up and said he knew he had a cabin in Idaho. They had gone on a fishing trip there once. Jim asked where exactly is it. Kevin said it was up near Lake Pend Oreille in northern Idaho. The town we bought groceries at was Sandpoint. It was about ten miles north of there. I spoke up, "Would he go there in winter? Idaho has worst snowfall than what we just experienced."

Mike asked, "Is there another place he would go?"

Kevin said, "I know if I were him I would go to the cabin. The road into it isn't bad, and he has a four-wheel drive SUV at his mother's house in Sandpoint."

"Well," Jim said, "why didn't you mention his mother's place first? What is his mother's first name? Or do you happen to remember her address?" Kevin shook his head no on both counts. Mike was already on the phone calling a friend who worked for the Sandpoint Police Department. He had been listening and started asking his friend to be on the lookout for Carl Moore. There was an arrest warrant out for him in Seattle. When he hung up, he said Allen told him he knew Carl and his mother. They would have an unmarked car stationed a couple of block from her home.

I said, "Was he surprised about the warrant?" Mike said no and that made him suspicious. He must have done something there otherwise Allen would have asked what the warrant was for.

We went to lunch at a different restaurant now that we knew Carl had given out our favorite eating place. It was totally in a different direction, and we still looked over our shoulders. I was disappointed and so was Mike. I said, "We can scratch that one off our dining establishment list." Mike agreed wholeheartedly. We went back to the station hoping to hear good news.

Jim was on the phone when we entered the squad room. He had a smile on his face, so we hurried in there and waited to hear what the call was about. We were hoping it was about Carl's arrest. Jim confirmed that Carl was under arrest and would be transported back to Washington. Allen told me to tell Mike that he didn't even put up a fight. His mother, on the other hand, had to be subdued.

Mike laughed really hard. We all looked at him as if he were crazy. He said, "You don't know Allen. He was an army ranger, and I can't see anyone putting up a fight with him especially an older woman."

I asked, "How do you know he was a ranger?"

He said, "I was one, and we were in the same outfit in Iraq." All the squad room stood up and started to clap. He said, "Oh stop it." Everyone said he deserved it.

Then quiet Bob came up and said, "I was there too, and I have been trying to remember where I met you before. It was in Mosel. Our unit was surrounded and all of a sudden a helicopter came in dropping a bunch of rangers. You were one of them. You guys saved our butts. I always wanted to thank one of you personally and now I can."

Mike said, "I remembered you but didn't want to bring up some bad memories. You were wounded pretty bad, and I carried you to the helicopter." Bob extended his hand and Mike shook it. Then Bob gave him a big man hug.

Everyone had a tear in their eye. I really wanted to hug him too but contained myself. Maybe I'll do it when everyone isn't around. After everyone settled down, Bob said, "If it weren't for you guys, I wouldn't be standing here." Mike just nodded and smiled.

CHAPTER FIFTEEN

....

Wilbur and Randy

TO CHANGE THE SCENE, Jim said, "Let's get ready to welcome Carl back with a not-so-welcome homecoming." At that moment, a call came in from Officer Jeff. He said they had a tip about a vacant house being broken into. The description given sounded a lot like Wilbur and Randy, the two men we were looking for. Jim said, "Get there, but not too close. We are on the way."

The house was in the Fremont district on a street near the troll statue. The troll sits under the Aurora Bridge, and it is a favorite with locals as well as visitors. Why it was put there is a mystery to me, but I love it.

We headed north out of the city with sirens blaring. The closer we got, we were turned them off. We crossed the Fremont bridge and made our way to the areas and surrounded the house. There was a SWAT team and several officers in the contingent. Jim took pleasure in getting on the bullhorn and requesting they give themselves up. Shots rang out from the house.

Jim gave the okay for a responding volley. It came from all different directions. Then there was silence. Jim yelled into the bullhorn, "Throw out your weapons and come out with your hands up." A "hell no" came from the house. Jim responded with, "We have enough firepower out here to bring that house down. I don't think you want to die there." Silence hung for a couple of minutes then weapons started pouring out of the house. They had about seven different handguns, a couple of rifles, and one assault rifle. They must have planned to hold up in there long before the tip came in. I was sure the neighbors were glad all this hubbub was done before an innocent person was hurt. So were we.

After they were booked, we took them straight to interrogation. Jim and Jeff took pleasure in being able to question Randy. Mike and I got Wilbur since we had previously been in contact with him. Plus, Mike was bigger than him.

We walked into the room, and Wilbur glared at us and said, "I'm not talking especially to that stupid c——t."

Mike stood over him and said, "You will talk decently or you won't be talking for a very long time." The look on his face was enough to scare me. Wilbur hung his head and whispered okay. Mike sat down and said, "If you are the first one to give us good information, your length of sentencing will probably be shortened."

Wilbur looked at him and said, "Randy won't say a word."

I said, "Are you sure? I can go in that room, listen, then come back and let you know what tune he is singing.

He said, "Shut up you—" And before he got the rest of the sentence out, Mike was out of his chair standing over him. He shrunk about three inches.

Mike growled, "Speak now or it's back to your cell with you."

Wilbur weakly said, "What do you want to know?"

Mike asked how he got tied up with Mr. Douglas. Wilbur replied they met in Texas. "Randy and I were known for taking care of unwanted people. Mr. Douglas hired us to kill a drug dealer who had cheated him. He told us he wanted to send the other dealers a message. Mr. Douglas told us exactly how we were to kill him and where to put his body. We did it, but the law was on our tail right away. Someone recognized us placing the body in front of another dealer's home. Mr. Douglas told us he could use our services up in Washington state. He put us on his private plane and we were gone."

I asked, "What services have you provided up here?"

Wilbur glared but knew he better answer. He said, "We roughed up some local dealers who were doing business on their own. They came on board with Mr. Douglas. We took turns keeping track of the Wilde Company business. Mr. Wilde was a wild card, as Mr. Douglas put it. During that time, we noticed a young lady snooping around. Mr. Douglas told us he had someone else to take care of her. I asked and who was that. Moe, he replied."

"Did he also have Rita taken care of?"

"Mr. Douglas wanted Moe too do her too."

"Did you take care of Duncan Olson?" Mike asked.

"Yah, he was too much for Moe to handle. That little weasel would have gotten the shit beaten out of him if he tried that." I asked who authorized that killing. "Mr. Douglas," he replied.

My final questions was how is Susan Hastings tied up in this mess.

He said, "She was the person giving orders for Mr. Douglas. He told us to do whatever she said. She was his second in command."

Mike's final question was, "Who ordered you to kill Amy and me?"

Wilbur said that it was just business, and "Mr. Douglas told us to tie up two more loose ends."

I said, "I have one more question. How did Officer Carl Moore fit into the picture?"

Wilbur said he knew him when he lived in Sandpoint, Idaho. "I heard he was a cop here, and Randy and I approached him. I told him if he didn't give us the information we wanted, we would have his mother killed. To add a little icing to the cake, I knew he had a record in Sandpoint for robbing a store as a minor. I said I would be obliged to let the police department know this little fact."

"How did he react?"

"He said the only way he was going to give us info was for a lot of money."

"How much did you give him?" I asked.

"He only got ten thousand. We than planted another ten thousand and a bag of drugs in his house in case he backed out."

I said, I think we have all the information we need." I called to the officer guarding the door that Wilbur could be taken to his cell now.

We met Jim and Jeff in the hallway and asked if they were successful in getting Randy to talk. They said he sang but didn't give much useful info. Mike looked at me and smiled. Jim said, "Give!" We told him everything Wilbur said minus the cuss word directed at me. Mike said it was all on tape. This will definitely put all of them in prison. Maybe get Mr. Douglas all the way to the death chamber.

I said, "I am going to call the Clumps and tell them we kept our promise and have all the people responsible for their daughter's murder."

Mike said, "I'm going to be there too. They deserve having some good news. I don't think any of them will be able to get out of being convicted by a jury for all they have done. Especially with all the evidence we have against them."

"After we go tell the Clumps, I would like to call Ruby to let her know we have confessions for the murder of her brother and Victoria. She can pass the information on to all the people at TWC," I said. "I know the ladies, Nicole, Claire, Sarah, and Carl will be very happy to have this news.

Jim put in his two cents and said, "I'm waiting for our Carl to get here. I want to hear him say he ratted on his fellow police officers for money. That lowlife. I can't believe he was a such a different person than what he showed us while he was in the squad room."

I said, "I know what you mean. Tell him I didn't enjoy being shot at and tracked down like an animal." Mike said ditto.

We went to our desks. I dialed the phone at my desk and put it on speaker so Mike could hear the conversation. Mrs. Clump answered on the third ring, and I said, "Hello, this is Detective Amy and Detective Mike."

He said, "We have you on speakerphone, so we can tell you together." At the same time, we told her, "We have all the people responsible for Victoria's murder in custody and all the information to have them in prison for a very long time."

She started to cry and Mr. Clump came on the line saying, "What is going on?" We told him the same thing, and by his voice, I knew he was struggling to keep the tears from coming. Finally, he said thank you.

I said, "I always keep my promises, especially this one. I would never have given up on finding the person or persons responsible."

I then asked if they were planning a memorial or funeral for Victoria, and he said, "I will let Mary tell you as she has been working on it." Mrs. Clump came on the line and gave us the details. She said, "Thank you from the bottom of my heart. I knew when I said promise me you will find them, that you would do everything to keep it."

I said, "At that time, I told myself it was a promise I would keep." We then said we will be at the service and hung up. We forgot to get the information about the memorial. That we could do later. We have another call to make now.

I said, "Mike, please call Ruby to let her know. I think I have talked as much as I want to for a while." He smiled and dialed her number. He told her exactly what we had said to the Clumps except it was for Duncan's murder. She was crying, and we could hear her mother in the background crying. She thanked him and he asked about the service for Duncan. She said he was going to be interned at Evergreen Washelli Cemetery. It was the same day as Victoria's in the same cemetery but a few minutes later. I asked if she knew Victoria was being buried there too on the same day. She said yes; she had coordinated it with Mrs. Clump so everyone could attend both. Then there will be a memorial at Anthony's Home Port in Ballard following the services. Anthony's will be closed to the public, so everyone invited can attend. She added it will be overflowing with all the co-workers, family, and many friends. She added, "Unbeknownst to me, Mary Clump was an old friend of my mother's. Mary's mother and father are buried near Poppa. So her daughter and my brother will be near them too."

Mike said, "Amy and I will be there as we promised you." He said, "I'm glad you contacted Mrs. Clump to make this possible." She said thanks and hung up.

Mike was hanging his head, and I knew he was thinking of his own father's internment. I put my hand on his shoulder and said, "Do you want me to make the call to the funeral parlor and tell them we are ready for his service?"

He looked up, and there were tears in his eyes. He put his hand over mine and said, "Let's do it together just like we did the last two." He dialed and told Mr. Reed he wanted to have the service tomorrow morning. Mr. Reed said would it be alright if it was at 11:00 a.m. as there was another one scheduled at 9:30 a.m. Mike and I said that would be fine as I had nodded in agreement. We didn't know Jim had been watching us when he said what was that all about. I explained that Mike's dad had passed away the night after we started the investigation into Victoria's death. He was just setting up his internment.

Jim looked at Mike and said, "Why didn't you tell me? I could have had another detective help Amy with the case."

Mike looked at him and said, "I wanted to work. Amy knew about it and said she would keep my mind off of his passing. She did just that. She is going to go with me as my dad wanted her there."

Jim asked if it would be alright if he was there too. He liked Mr. Bowers a lot, which Mike knew. Mike nodded and said, "My dad would have like you to be there too."

Jim said, "11:00 a.m. at?"

Mike said, "Washilli of course. He wanted to be next to mother and that is where he is going to be."

I looked at Mike and said, "Do you want to blow this joint?"

He laughed and said, "Hell yes. I'm taking you to the best place in town for dinner."

I said, "Where is that?"

He laughed and said, "At the hole-in-the-wall."

Vivian met us at the door and said, "You didn't bring another welcoming party, did you?"

We laughed and said, "No, they are all in jail. We are celebrating." She gave us a high-five and showed us to the corner table. She told us the special was steak, baked potato, grilled asparagus, a salad, and a roll. We said bring it on.

Mike whispered, "I know this isn't that special."

I said, "Well, it is special for us." He smiled. Along with the dinner, Vivian brought over a very nice Merlot. We ate and drank our wine leisurely. We enjoyed not having to look at the door every few minutes.

When we were done, Vivian came over and said, "This dinner is on the house."

I said, "Won't you get in trouble with the owner?"

She smiled and said, "I am the owner."

"Well, I'll be darned," I said.

She laughed and said, "I like to have direct contact with my customers. You guys are my favorites."

We said, "You are our favorite too, and I gave her a big hug."

She said to Mike, "Take this beautiful young lady home. She deserves a good rest."

Mike grinned and said, "I planned on taking her home but maybe not for a good rest." Vivian swatted him on the backside and smiled.

I was blushing, and when we got outside, I said, "What exactly do you have planned?"

He looked at me and said, "Just wait and see."

I told him, "I'm a very impatient person."

He said, "I know, but you will have to wait for this."

Oh brother, I figured I was in for it whatever it was. I was pleasantly surprised. In my apartment was a dozen red roses, a bottle of champagne chilling, candlelight, and music. I said, "This is wonderful." He turned me around and gave me a warm soft kiss. The rest of the night will be forever in my heart.

The next morning, we arrived at Washilli and Jim was waiting. We followed the cemetery director to Mr. Bowers's plot. The minister from Mike's fathers church was there and the three of us. We listened as the minister gave his wonderful speech about Mr. Bowers. Mike than put a rose by his urn, I followed, and Jim laid his rose on the pedestal. Then Mike asked Jim if he and I could have a moment. He walked some ways away. Mike leaned over to the urn and said, "Dad, Amy and I are going to be married." I had my mouth open to say something and out popped a yes. The sun came out and it was like his dad was giving his blessing. Jim came over put his arm around us and said, "I approve too."

We both beamed. I was thinking this is just the beginning and threw my arms around Mike and kissed him for all I was worth.

ABOUT THE AUTHOR

....

AS A TEENAGER, I discovered the joy of reading mysteries. Eventually, it became my desire to write my own book. When I retired, I realized the book was still rolling around in my head. It was time to set the wheels in motion and accomplish my desire. I loved every minute while writing the mystery. I hope you will enjoy reading it as much as I did writing it.

CPSIA information can be obtained
at www.ICGtesting.com
Printed in the USA
FSHW010147260421
80725FS